The Story of Faith

By

Kevin Wright

The Story of Faith

By Kevin Wright

This is a work of fiction. Names, characters, places, incidents and events are the product of the author's imagination or are used fictitiously. Any resemblance to actual persons, living or dead, or actual events, is purely coincidental.

Copyright © 2019 by Kevin Wright. All rights reserved.
Published in the United States of America.

Cover design by Alexandria Melone
Edited by Nick May at TypeRight, LLC

Contact the author at kewererory@aol.com

ISBN 978-1-7333151-0-4

FIRST EDITION

Have faith in your purpose.
Enjoy the small and beautiful things
that make up everyday life.
Life is messy.
It's full of setbacks and disappointments.
We lose things we can't get back.
Push forward for there is a reason you are here.

Chapter 1: Brenda Jones

"This is 911. What's your emergency?"

"I'm having trouble seeing and I'm very dizzy and can't stand up."

"Stay on the line, I'm contacting emergency personnel. Keep talking to me. What's your name? Ma'am, what's your name?"

She was having trouble gathering her thoughts. "Uh, this is Brenda."

"Brenda, what's your last name?"

"Jones, this is Brenda Jones."

"Ms. Jones, just stay where you are."

"No, I have to get something from my nightstand. I must get it. It's for my daughter."

"Ms. Jones, what's your daughter's name?"

"Who?"

"Your daughter. What's her name?"

"Faith is my daughter. I must get something to give my daughter. I can't seem to get to my room. My body is not working right. I think I'm going to black out."

"Ms. Jones, stay where you are. Ms. Jones? Brenda? Stay on the phone. Are you there?"

*

Brenda had been to the doctor before about her headaches and had scheduled a day for an MRI, but her symptoms had gotten the best of her this morning. The doctors had spent most of the morning running tests. She was finally back in her room, and she texted Faith. She didn't want to alarm her daughter, so the text was lacking in detail: *"At the hospital had some tests run. I will need a ride home."*

Doctor Suresh entered her room. She was wearing a typical white coat. "Ms. Jones, is there anybody here with you?"

Brenda took that moment in. She was anxious. *What did the doctor find?* The anticipation sent adrenaline running through her body and made her lightheaded. What came next could be about her future, if there was to be one. It could be a difficult road or a clear path forward—or no road at all, a dead end. She considered the question, the body language of the doctor, and her expression and set her expectation for what was coming. There would be no clear path, only a difficult road or a dead end. "My daughter will be here shortly," Brenda replied. "I should have called her earlier, but I wanted to get all the testing completed before she showed up." She took a deep breath and cleared her mind to accept the news at hand. "My intuition tells me you have some bad news."

The doctor hesitated; Brenda knew there would be no good news for her today, or for that matter, anytime going forward.

"Go on, I can handle it."

The doctor moved closer, pulled up a chair, and took her hand. "Ms. Jones, you have a tumor inside your head. It's applying pressure in areas that are causing your side effects. It's rather large and intertwined with your brain. It's in an area where even a biopsy is dangerous. Without a biopsy, it's hard to know what type of cancer we are dealing with. The unknowns are my real concern."

"Do you have any good news for me?" Brenda asked.

The doctor contemplated the question briefly, "Good news? Hmm, we might be able to slow its progression and lessen the side effects it is causing. We will have to do radiation, which will help us determine the response the tumor will have, and this will give us an idea of what we are dealing with."

"I see." Brenda hesitated. "I hadn't ruled out this possibility. When you say you can subdue the side effects with treatment, does this mean the treatments are side-effect free?"

"Well, Ms. Jones, I can't promise that."

The hospital room door creaked open with a slight knock. "Hey, Mom, why didn't you tell me you were coming to the hospital?" Faith asked as she stepped into the room.

Brenda pulled her hand from the doctor, and the doctor stood up. "Doctor Suresh, this is my daughter, Faith."

"Very nice to meet you, Dr. Suresh," Faith replied.

"Dr. Suresh was just leaving," Brenda said. "Thank you for stopping by, Doctor. We can finish our conversation later."

"Sure, Ms. Jones. I'll let you and your daughter visit." Dr. Suresh exited the room.

"Mom, what's going on? Why didn't you tell me you were feeling bad?"

"You have plenty to worry about without having to keep up with my everyday affairs."

"Well, I wouldn't consider a visit to the hospital a routine part of day-to-day life." Faith was exasperated at her mother's laissez-faire attitude. "Maybe a visit to the doctor's office, but not the hospital. So, Mom, what's going on?" Faith sat in the chair the doctor had just vacated.

Faith was accustomed to being part of her mom's mysteries. She often withheld pertinent details from Faith, and it took time and persistent questioning to pull the whole story out of her.

"Well, Faith, I have been having headaches and dizzy spells, and some blurred vision, so my primary care doctor, Dr. Williams, scheduled me for some tests."

Faith stammered to get the next question out, and it turned into a multiple-choice list. "Mom, what . . . when did this first start? How bad . . . how long has it been going? How bad are the headaches . . . and the dizzy spells? And how did you get here if you have blurred vision?" Faith paused. "What did the doctor say?"

"They are not sure how bad it is, but they have a plan to help alleviate some of my symptoms."

Faith's anxiety subsided for a minute. "Well that's good. Wait, how bad what is? What's causing this? Do you have cancer?" With that last question, Faith's emotions started to kick in. She had not started crying, but the tears were building, and she had to clear her throat.

Brenda hesitated. "Faith, we will deal with this, good or bad, but we don't know what we are dealing with yet. Don't cry. You are going to make me cry."

Faith wiped her eyes before her tears began running down her checks. "Mom, I love you. You are right. We will get through this, but I need to know what we are dealing with. I need to know if you will be here for me." Faith paused, exasperated with herself. "What am I saying? I will be here for you. That's what I'm saying: I will be here for you."

"I know you will, my beautiful. I have thrown a real right hook at you. I'm sorry, Faith. I have always tried to protect you and shield you from my transgressions and escapades. I didn't want to cause you any undue anxiety until I knew what I was dealing with."

"Thanks, Mom. I know you are always looking out for my best interests."

Brenda took the opportunity to change the subject. "Speaking of your best interests, how is that fool you are dating, and where is he?"

"He dropped me off. He has a campaign rally to be at."

"That's the best news I've had today!" Brenda said.

"Mom! You know he could be the next congressman for this area. You need to be nice."

"I have been dealing with his kind for all thirty years of your life. Don't get me wrong, they helped us survive, but I wanted to live. I wanted you to live, and not just survive. I got tired of those tiny handouts and decided to seek my own route. Did I ever tell you about the moment that I knew that we were just surviving, and not living?"

Faith shook her head.

"I had just picked up our government check and went down to the basement of that old city-services building to find a restroom. As I was walking down a long hallway, there was an older lady down at the end of the hall. She was digging around in her cleaning cart and humming to herself. We were the only two people in that long hallway. As I passed her, she stopped her humming.

"She asked, 'Why do you have your head down, my darling?'

"I just smiled and said, 'Hello.'

"'You know darling, if you walk around with your head down, you will never see life's possibilities. Stand up tall and look at what's in front of you. Only vision can guide you, and you won't see that by looking at the dirt.'

"I smiled at her and went on into the restroom. When I came back out, neither she nor her cleaning cart were to be found.

"That evening, after I had put you to bed, I was looking at my reflection in the bathroom mirror. That moment came back to me. Was I not happy? Was I settling and limiting not only my life, but yours? Why wait for handouts? Why not seek a better life?

"Next year came and you started pre-K, and I went to work. That's when we started living! I will never forget that short chance encounter with the old cleaning lady. I never let a bad day get in the way of my appreciation for what I had.

"I have you, and that's all I ever need."

"Mom, that's a great story—you never told me that."

"I wish I could have given you more," Brenda lamented. "I wish you could have known your dad."

"Mom, you gave me so much. You have always had all the love and caring I needed."

Faith's cell phone rang, interrupting the mood. "It's George." Faith answered and stood up. "Hey, how is the rally going?" Faith asked as she stepped out into the hall.

It didn't appear to Brenda that the phone call was going well. Then it ended suddenly, and Faith was back in the room. "How is George?" Brenda asked.

"He's mad. He wanted me to be there."

"Did he ask about me?"

"Mom, no, but he is really busy and distracted by this campaign. He got mad when I told him I was going to stay here with you tonight."

"Is that right?"

"Mom, he's a good guy!"

Brenda hesitated and thought better of speaking ill of George again, but she was never one to hold back her thoughts. "Faith, you don't commit to relationships because somebody is a good guy, and by the way, I disagree with your assessment of his character. We left so many of our friends behind because of politicians like him. I had to get us out of that cycle of relying on another's good will. They promise the world and deliver crumbs. They only need us when it comes time for votes. I wish I could make people see that, but they keep electing the same George. I got more from that cleaning lady in ten seconds than I have ever gotten from all those politicians combined."

"Well, maybe you should run for office," Faith quipped.

"It's not in the cards. I just want you to know how I feel. Be careful of those who promise the stars, and then the next year, they promise the stars, again!"

Dr. Suresh knocked on the door and entered. "I have Misty with me. She will be taking you to your car so that you can return home tonight. I will only allow this if you promise me three things: First, you will ride in the wheelchair. Second, you will be at my office tomorrow afternoon. And last, you will have your daughter at the wheel."

Brenda took no time to accept these terms. She had been in the hospital all day. "Faith, will you drive me home?"

"Of course, Mom." Faith exited the hospital room and had her phone out before the door closed behind her.

"Ms. Jones, if you haven't already, it would be best if you and your daughter discuss your situation," said Doctor Suresh. "We will need to make some decisions tomorrow about your treatment options, and it's best that those who love you have a say. I wish I had more to offer, Ms. Jones. I will do my best to preserve your time and comfort going forward." With that, Doctor Suresh exited the room.

Brenda turned to the nurse. "She's not much on beating around the bush. What's your name again, honey?"

"I'm Misty. Can I help you with your clothes?"

"Please, honey. I never looked good in these gowns. They show too much of my heinie, and there is not much to see back there."

Brenda got in the wheelchair and they headed towards the front driveway of the hospital. It was the first moment she had to collect her thoughts, without Faith or Doctor Suresh around. Tears built as she thought of herself moving on. She thought about how much she would miss her daughter. She wondered if her daughter was ready to take care of herself, and if the dependence they had built together was well-served. She quickly wiped the tears away and moved to better thoughts. She thought of the great life they had together . . . the good times. Faith was finishing her art degree. Brenda thought how wonderful to have been given the time to see her finish her degree, but she knew that she couldn't leave Faith without a backup plan. She had very little trust in George, and she needed to come clean about something she had hidden from Faith all these years. She knew it would be a dangerous topic this late in the game, but she trusted in her daughter's love and understanding, and besides, it could be a great adventure and distraction for Faith once Brenda was gone.

Faith was in the drive waiting when Misty pushed Brenda's wheelchair out the front door. Misty helped her in the front passenger seat and was back in the hospital before they started their departure.

Brenda could tell Faith was upset. She guessed it was the phone call she'd made as she was leaving the hospital room, and it was probably to George.

The Story of Faith

Faith tried to hide it by bringing up the turn of events of her driving her mom home, after so many years of mom being her transportation. They joked about that, but after a few minutes, they both got quiet.

"George is such a dick!" Faith blurted out.

"Why? What happened?"

"He is at one of his fundraisers tonight and wanted me to be there. He is meeting with several corporate donors, and he likes me to be by his side for these meetings."

Brenda asked, "What kind of people donate to his campaign?"

"Mainly big corporations. They really need help with labor cost. They have many low-level jobs that we Americans just won't do. That's one of George's campaign priorities."

"That's very noble of him," said Brenda. "How will he help all those people in our old neighborhood?"

"His plan is to help them by working with the federal government to make sure they have a safety net. It's so hard to find good-paying jobs these days." Faith, realizing how stupid, conflicting, and demeaning she sounded, stopped talking, a little embarrassed by her own thoughts.

Chapter 2:
No Good News

Brenda awoke to the smell of brewing coffee. The aroma brought back memories of her childhood. What she missed about times past were the aromas and sounds related to breakfast. The door was shut, keeping the sound of cooking down, but she could still make out the sound of the old percolator brewing coffee. How soothing that sound was. It kept you hypnotized just enough to get a little more sleep.

She had slept well last night. The previous day's activities had been mentally taxing, not to mention physically demanding. It didn't take much activity these days to tire her. She figured it was related to her current health issues. That realization bought her mind to full attention. She had to level with Faith, and it had to be before today's doctor visit.

"Faith?" Brenda yelled from her bed. "Will you be serving me breakfast in bed this morning?" She laughed to herself with that question.

"I sure can, Mom."

Brenda couldn't resist one more chance to chide her daughter. "In that case, can I have fresh-squeezed orange juice, sausage, and biscuits . . . gravy would be nice, and some poached eggs?"

Her bedroom door flew open. "Mom, seriously? I have never seen you eat *any* of that stuff, and besides the one ingredient I have to fill that order is the milk that would go towards the gravy."

Brenda smiled. "Well, I guess I will have the usual. Cereal, please . . . and I'm kidding about having it in bed. I want to sit with you this morning."

Brenda made her way to the table.

"I can make that breakfast for you in the morning if you would like," Faith said.

"Thank you dear, but I was just kidding. I never really liked breakfast. I enjoy what it meant to me when I was a kid. The freshness of new a day, adventures to come, the thought of my mom taking care of me, and sitting down with them ... my mom and dad, whether much was said or not. Faith, our mornings were so busy we really didn't have time for a production. Besides, I wanted the time with my little girl in the mornings. I'm so thankful I took the time and still have the memories of you sitting in your highchair with just a diaper on, spooning that cereal up, milk running down your chin and all down your stomach."

Faith jumped in. "I remember Pop-Tarts!"

Brenda laughed. "Yes, Pop-Tarts came when you started going to school."

"They just don't taste as good as they did when I was a kid. Mom, why didn't we spend more time with Granny and Pappy?"

"I owe you an explanation, Faith. You have asked many times. I will explain why when the time is right. Let's drop it for now."

Brenda paused. "Let's cook supper here tonight. Just liked we used to. We can make some of our old favorites like Hamburger Helper or goulash. I can make some mash potatoes and corn, and you can mix them together liked you used to do. Which would you prefer, Hamburger Helper or goulash?"

"I think . . . " Faith paused while she carefully weighed her choices. "Goulash!"

"Oh Faith, that's my favorite, too."

That happy moment was followed by silence, and Brenda's smile slowly turned into sadness, as tears blurred her vision. She finally blinked and washed away the tears, which now ran down her cheeks.

"Oh, Mom," was all Faith could say, as she was also overcome with emotion.

Brenda was trying to come up with the words to explain her situation. *How can you tell someone you are dying but not upset them?* she thought. *You can't,* she decided, *and, besides, the tears already set the stage.* Brenda took the palm of her hand and wiped her tears away.

"Faith, I'm dying." The finality of those two words brought her emotions back in check. *There! I admitted and accepted it in one fail swoop.* "I have a tumor in my head, and it's causing all my issues. Doctor Suresh is not sure what we are dealing with, but she knows she cannot operate. That leaves radiation. The radiation treatment should give us some idea how fast it's growing. Depending on that, we will have some idea how much time I have left."

Faith sat in front of her mom with tears running down her face, just as raindrops would on a window. Without a word, she got up and walked around to the back of her mom's chair and wrapped her arms around her. She held on to her mom for several minutes. Faith finally was able to let go and gather herself. She took a seat beside her. "Mom let's see what the doctor says today, and we will take that information and make the best of it."

Brenda finished her cereal as Faith looked on. Both missed the irony of the role reversal from so many years earlier when Faith was in the highchair.

Brenda looked up. "Let's make that grocery list and get on with the day."

They had just enough time to unpack the groceries before heading to Doctor Suresh's office. Faith once again took the wheel of the car, and the trip proved uneventful.

Once in the office, they checked in and sat down to wait their turn. Brenda wondered about the other people in the waiting room. What were they battling? What did the future hold for them?

Faith had different thoughts. She was nervous about the news she was about to tackle. She was apprehensive about the treatment and side effects that her mom would endure. She was frightened about the time that was left on her mom's clock. It was not a setting that Faith would wish upon anybody. Yet here she was, within just 24 hours of hearing about any issues, dealing with so much uncertainty about what lay ahead.

"Ms. Jones, we are ready for you."

The butterflies in Faith's stomach were not just creating anxiety; she was really nauseated. She took a few deep breaths as her mom went through the check-in process: height, weight, temperature, and blood pressure. They were finally seated in Doctor Suresh's office.

The Story of Faith

"Doctor Suresh will be with you shortly."

Not much was said as they both sat there waiting. Brenda finally broke the silence. "I'm already getting hungry just thinking about dinner tonight."

At that moment, all Faith could do was agree, but her stomach was telling a completely different story.

"Faith, adding birthday cake to our grocery list was a great idea. Let's celebrate life—our life." Brenda could sense her daughter's uneasy state. "Faith, always remember this. There are things in life that you can control and things you cannot. This thing I'm dealing with—it's beyond our control. It's in God's hands now. Let's take what we are dealt and make the best of it."

Doctor Suresh entered the room. Instead of sitting behind her desk, she leaned against the front of it, facing Faith and Brenda. Doctor Suresh paused briefly before she spoke. "Ms. Jones, Faith, thank you for coming in today. Ms. Jones, have you told your daughter about what you are dealing with?"

"I have," Brenda replied.

No Good News

Doctor Suresh continued. "When I visit with patients, and I have all the answers, I sit behind my desk. It's because I'm confident that I have all the answers and a plan to defeat the invader they are fighting. I'm also confident that plan—treatment, if you will—will provide time for them and those who care about them. I'm not sitting behind my desk. I'm standing in front of you because I'm not sure. I'm not sure if the treatment will help. I'm not sure how this invader will respond to my plan. Most concerning, I'm not sure how much time your mom has, Faith." She knelt in front of Brenda and Faith and took the hand of each. "Therefore, I'm here to let you know we will do everything we can to figure this out." Doctor Suresh paused before standing back up. "Enough of my thoughts. What questions do you have for me?"

Faith was first to speak. "What can I do to help?"

"You are doing it! Be here for your mom. Be here for her appointments. Be here for her treatments. Be here for her. If there are other family members Ms. Jones wants involved, reach out to them. If we can make progress with this enemy, then get involved with a support group. Ms. Jones, do you have any questions?"

Brenda paused a minute. "What's your plan, when do we get started, and what kind of side effects will I have?"

Nothing Brenda heard was appealing. Cancer is an ugly disease and so is the battle.

They were about to leave when Faith posed one last question. "Do you have any other advice for us?"

Doctor Suresh thought a minute. "Don't let this deter your confidence that we will do everything in our power to help your mom, but take the time to talk. It's never too late to shore up the family business affairs and to talk about anything that has been left unsaid."

Brenda was once again reminded that she must come clean with Faith.

Chapter 3: George

Faith was cleaning up from a memorable dinner. It was memorable because it bought back all the times she and her mom had sat at that very table and enjoyed the very same favorite things. She remembered how much life and living had taken place at that very table over the years. Faith wanted this meal to be one she could look back on in the future and remember the many things she and her mom had shared. There were the school projects they worked on together, the homework, the birthdays, her friends of past and present, the trips to the park, and even camping on occasion. They had tried girl scouts, but it hadn't worked out—and a laundry list of sports, dance, and cheerleading. Faith thought about all those things and how much she loved each one of them, but the time and expense had been too much.

As she dried and returned the dishes to the cabinet, she thought about her future, her kids, how she would love them, and how nice it would be to have a husband who was there to help, love, and care for their kids. Her kids would get to do those things she'd missed out on. They would all be together for holidays. They could all take off for the beach, or sit around the Christmas tree, or have a turkey dinner at Thanksgiving. She longed to experience those winter holidays she'd only glimpsed when she was growing up. Her mom always tried to have friends visit on those holidays, but most of the time they were the ones doing the visiting. It meant so much to see how her mom's friends gathered and enjoying the time together. They talked often about how lucky they were to have friends that welcomed them as part of their family during those celebrations.

George

As she put the last dish away and turned to her mom, Faith found she had fallen asleep on the couch. Knowing what her mom was dealing with, she had a fleeting moment of concern, but as she drew closer, she could see she was still breathing, her chest moving slowly up and down.

Though that moment was over in an instant, it stuck with her till deep in the night. As she lay in bed, she was inundated with a million concerns. Was she ready to be independent? Could it be that she would soon be alone in this world? When her mom passed, she would have only her friends, who were themselves quickly transitioning into their own career and families. Would she have George? She had her doubts. Not only was she concerned about the lack of a safety net, she had no idea of life beyond today. She did have a degree, and that started her mind thinking about things she could do. Finally, her mind slowed down and let her go to sleep.

Brenda was at the table having coffee when Faith entered the kitchen. "You look wonderful. Did you sleep well last night?"

Faith grabbed a glass and went to the fridge for juice. "I did, Mom. How was the couch last night?"

"It must have been good—I slept through the night. It looks like you might be going somewhere today?"

Faith took a sip of her orange juice before replying. "George has a campaign rally today. He has been bugging me to go for several days. I don't have to go, Mom. I can stay here with you."

Brenda was quick to reply. "Nonsense! Go on to that rally with George. I'll be OK. Do you need my car?"

Faith took another sip and hesitated. "George is picking me up. Are you sure you will be OK? Do you need me to do anything for you?"

"I'm fine."

"Can I pick anything up for you while I'm out?"

"I don't really need anything. What time do you think you will be back? If it's around dinner time, can you pick up some fast food?"

Faith sat down at the table. "I'll be back by dinner. How about Chick-fil-A?"

Brenda didn't have to think twice before answering. "Sure! Bring me one of their chocolate chip cookies. Get some money out of my purse."

"Mom! I got this. I can afford to pick up Chick-fil-A for us."

Faith picked up the sports section of the newspaper from the kitchen table. Brenda went back to thumbing through the other sections. As she rifled through the pages, Brenda found nothing that really interested her. She wasn't really looking at the paper. She was trying to decide how to begin the conversation that had dwelled in her thoughts for way too many years. Another dilemma—just as when she'd had to break the news about her brain tumor. She could not get her thoughts gathered to start the conversation, so she just kept rifling through the newspaper. She stopped flipping the pages finally and landed in the wedding and engagement section. "Faith. Look at this beautiful couple." She laid the paper down in front of Faith. "Back when I was young, this was taboo. It was frowned upon. That outrage came from both sides.

It didn't matter if you were black, white, red, or green, it was forbidden. It's so good to see that most people now look beyond skin color. It's seen for what it is: two people who are in love. Your grandmother and grandfather were that way. It's one of the reasons I had such an estranged relationship with them." Before Brenda could continue, the moment was interrupted by a car horn, honking from outside.

Faith stood up from the table. "That must be George! Are you sure you will be OK?"

"I'll be OK as long as you don't forget my cookie from Chick-fil-A!" The horn honked again.

"He must be in a hurry," Faith said, trying to excuse the behavior of George. Faith leaned over and kissed her mom on the forehead and was off.

Brenda could tell she was about to lite into George, politician, or not.

Faith ran out of the house and climbed into the open passenger door. "George, what the hell!"

"What? I'm running late," exclaimed George as he drove off.

George

"You want to represent the people of this community and manage their well-being, and you can't even plan a trip to your campaign rally?"

"Politicians are notoriously late; it's not a big deal."

Faith fumed at that response. "Are you kidding? Maybe that is why they are so disliked. And maybe, that's why most people never bother to vote! What bothers me most is, it's OK to be late, but you couldn't take the time to come in and say something to Mom? When you know what she is facing? It's disgusting and disappointing." The tears started rolling. She hated crying when she was mad. She didn't want sympathy—she wanted understanding. The combination of emotional distress and lack of empathy from George brought on a flood of tears, and she couldn't stop it.

"George, maybe I shouldn't go. I don't know how supportive I can be for you right now."

George pulled over to the side of the road. "I need you there with me. Having you there gives me confidence and comfort.

I'm more relaxed and surer of what I'm saying and doing. I know you are struggling with your mom's situation, but share a little time with me today. I promise to make it up to you."

Faith collected herself and decided to move forward. "Ok, George, but I need to be back by evening. I promised Mom I would return with dinner."

Faith did enjoy these functions. She enjoyed the people and their loyalty and support of George. She saw another side of George when he was interacting with his constituents. She saw empathy and understanding for the plight of those he wished to represent.

George took the stage to cheers and applause. It was his tradition to invite Faith on stage at the end. Today would be no different. "I have to introduce you to someone very special to me," he said. "She has been by my side since we started this journey and has been a big supporter of what I want to do for you and this community, and she is the love of my life. Please welcome my very own superstar, Faith!"

She and George spent the next hour mingling with the crowd of supporters. As the crowds dwindled, George was approached by two well-dressed businessmen. "Faith, this Paul and Ryan. They are two of my big donors."

The taller of the two spoke first. "I'm Ryan. It is nice to finally meet the rock that supports this fool. Is he crazy to be doing this?"

Before Faith could respond, the other spoke up. "George said you were beautiful, but even that description undercuts how truly stunning you are. I'm Paul." He shook her hand.

Ryan jumped back into the conversation. "George let's move this party over to Danny's. It's just down the street. We can grab some drinks and a snack. Can Faith please join us?"

"Well, of course she can," George replied.

"Well then, let's get a move on," Ryan suggested. "My car and driver are right over here."

"We will meet you there. I have my car here," George said.

Faith had seen this scene before. She enjoyed these kinds of meetings, but they could go on forever, and tonight she had promised her mom dinner. Dinner at a decent hour, for that matter. Instead, she was sitting in a restaurant at a booth with outdated décor. It reminded her of a '60s-style Italian restaurant with lattice work separating one row of tables from the neighboring row. It wasn't much for privacy. They could have talked with their neighbors through the lattice work, but the table was empty.

After appetizers, she excused herself to the restroom. The conversation had been interesting and entertaining, but she needed an excuse to break away. When she returned to the table, the conversation had turned into a discussion of campaign business. "Well, gentleman, it has been very nice meeting you, and thank you for your hospitality, but I must leave you boys to your business." Paul and Ryan both implored her to stay, but Faith stood firm. "I have a family commitment that I just have to keep."

"Would you mind taking an Uber?" George asked.

George

Ryan spoke up, "George, we can drop you off at your house if you would like Faith to drive your car."

George thought a minute. "That's a good idea, fellas. I have already had a few drinks."

"Well, it's settled then," Paul replied. "It was nice getting to know you. You are even more beautiful than George let on."

Not to be outdone, Ryan jumped in, "Not only do you have true beauty, but you're very smart and insightful, too. Maybe you should be running for office."

"You two are so sweet. Please take care of my candidate tonight, and make sure he gets home safely. Thanks again guys." With that, Faith gave George a kiss and was off.

She made it as far as the door before she realized George had not given her his car keys. She approached the booth from the opposite side. She had planned on just sticking her head through the lattice work and requesting the keys, but she stopped short when she heard the conversation was about her.

She could hear Paul speaking. "George, you have a beautiful girl . . . dark hair, dark eyes, smart—she is just amazing. What's her ethnicity?"

George was quick to respond, "Her mom is Black, but she has never mentioned her dad. My supporters are really drawn to her."

Ryan agreed. "She is a very sharp lady, and her ethnicity helps solidify the base we are after. We need that base to turn out and vote. We need a representative, such as yourself, to keep these folks supporting our interests. We need the labor force to keep production rolling. The only way to do that is to import the workers."

Paul concurred. "She is a very sharp lady and exudes confidence. She could be a good highlight on the campaign trail.

"What's her story? Where does she come from? She has such an appealing personality," Ryan said.

George thought for a second. "She overcame some great obstacles. Her mom had only graduated high school when she had Faith."

Paul jumped back in. "She fits the bill perfectly. She overcame single-parent upbringing, with the assistance of our wonderful country. She shows that the American dream is alive and well."

Faith was caught off guard. She was frozen in place. She appreciated the sentiment, but she felt like a tool. Not to mention, they had her and her mom's story all wrong. She was somewhat panicked. Should she stick her head through the trellis or rethink her entrance? She opted to come back around to the other side, so as not to create any suspicion that she'd been eavesdropping.

"George, I need the keys!" She realized the abrupt nature of her statement and tried again. "Sorry, the car won't start without the keys," she added with a half-smile.

George reached into his pocket and passed the car keys to her. "See you tonight."

Faith reminded him about dinner for her mom as she turned and walked away.

Chapter 4: Setting Sun

Faith had not seen George since he had come by to pick up his car. George was getting frustrated with her absence, and the pressure of the campaign was adding to his grumpiness. She started ignoring his phone calls to avoid the pressure that he was applying for her to be a part of the campaign.

Her mom was getting worse. The radiation therapy was not helping.

"Mom, you need to eat," implored Faith. "The last good meal you had was our dinner a few weeks ago."

Brenda took a minute to respond. "I'm so glad we had that meal together."

"We can do that again. I can cook you anything you want."

"My beautiful Faith, you are doing a wonderful job of taking care of me. Everything you have cooked has been my favorite, but I just don't feel like eating much." Brenda's movements had become increasingly labored, just as her speech seemed to be growing weaker and more difficult. This did not pass without concern from Faith.

"Mom?" Faith hesitated, trying not to get emotional. She cleared her throat and tried again. "Mom, I don't know what to do."

Brenda, having not lost her quick wit, responded, "You are doing it. You have picked up where my appetite has left off."

Faith found a smile. "Hmm, are you saying I'm gaining weight taking care of you?"

Brenda laughed. "I'm shrinking and you're growing." They both found a smile to share. "Faith, you are here for me. That's all I need. Just you, being here, so that I can focus on what a wonderful person and what a beautiful person you have turned out to be. This takes my mind off all the bad that is creeping over me. Thank you for that and thank you for reading to me. Now, instead of a book or newspaper today, can you get something else for me? Can you please go to the nightstand on the right side of the bed? The side I sleep on. In the bottom drawer, underneath my Bible, get the cookie tin and bring it to me. It's the holiday tin."

Faith made her way to her mom's bedroom. Her mom was very neat and was not a fan of clutter. Even in her declining condition, the room was still neatly kept. This room had been a haven for Faith when she was younger: storms, nightmares, and just hanging out with Mom on a Sunday afternoon. She found the Bible, which she and her mom often read, and underneath she found the cookie tin.

She headed back to the kitchen. "Mom, where did this come from? What's in it?" She entered the kitchen, but there was no response. What she saw stopped her dead in her tracks. Her mom was on the floor and appeared to be having a seizure. "Mom, Mom! What's happening?" She scooped her up in her arms in the middle of the kitchen floor and begin crying. "Mom, I'm going to call 911. Please don't leave me. Don't leave me, Mom. Don't leave. I'm going to get help."

*

The paramedics stabilized Brenda and loaded her in the ambulance.

"Ms. Jones?" one of the paramedics asked. Faith was not used to being called Ms. Jones. "Your mom wants to talk with you." Faith made haste toward the ambulance, not wanting to delay her mom's departure. "Mom, we need to get you to the hospital."

Brenda raised her hand. Faith knew she wanted quiet. Brenda motioned to Faith to come closer. Faith could see how weak she was. She could barely talk. Brenda was able to get out two words: "Cookie tin."

Not wanting to belabor the point, or further delay her mom's departure, she reassured her mom that she would bring it to the hospital.

*

It had been a long afternoon. Finally, Faith heard a nurse call for her. "Yes, I'm Ms. Jones."

"Please come with me." The nurse led her back to a consultation room. "Please wait here, Ms. Jones. The doctor will be with you shortly."

The nurse left Faith to imagine the worst. Perhaps her mom had not made it. She began to cry. She covered her face with her hands and leaned forward, with her elbows on her knees.

"Ms. Jones?" she heard from the doorway. A tall, slender man outfitted with a white hospital coat stood before her. "Would you like a tissue?" He extended his hand. "I'm Dr. Elliott. We have your mom stabilized. She is doing much better." Faith was very relieved. Dr. Elliott continued, "I have been in contact with Dr. Suresh. She has asked that we keep your mom overnight. She would like to see her, and perhaps run some additional test tomorrow. We are sure that the seizure your mom had today is directly related to the tumor in her head. This is an unforgiving disease, but unlike other types, it's not associated with a lot of pain or discomfort. We are in the process of moving her to a room. You are welcome to stay the night; my nurse will help with details. By the way, the medicine we have given her to keep the seizures at bay will keep her very sedated. Do you have any questions?"

Faith was exhausted from the emotional roller coaster of the last several hours. She thought for a moment, but her head was so cloudy she could come up with nothing. "No not at this time. Thank you very much, Dr. Elliott. Oh, yes! One question. Which room will she be in?"

Dr. Elliott stopped just short of the doorway. "Yes of course. Follow me, and I'll get our staff to get you where you need to go."

By the time Faith made it to the room, her mom was already there. A nurse stood out front. "Ms. Jones, I'm Betty. I will be the nurse in charge of your mom. I'm here until 6 a.m. If you need anything, just push this button. Are you planning on staying the night?"

"You can call me Faith. Yes, I think I will."

Betty reassured Faith, "We will take good care of Ms. Jones. Are you her daughter?" Faith never had the chance to answer. "I can see a remarkable similarity between you two. I'll bring in some bedding for you. Would you like anything to drink or eat? It's not a problem. I can call downstairs."

"No, I'm fine."

"Well, if you change your mind, let me know before 10 p.m." And with that, the nurse went on her way.

Faith pulled up a chair next to her mom's bed and placed her hands over Brenda's hands. She began praying for a miracle and wished she had bought the Bible with her when she'd left the house with the cookie tin. She thought about that small bit of irony, of moving the Bible to get to the cookie tin and the cascade of events that followed.

Faith started thinking about her mom, and she found herself drifting back to her childhood. She had so many great memories. Although their financial situation had not been the best. Her mom had always made the best of it, whether it was an amusement park or a day trip to the beach or forest.

Her mom had always made an adventure out of all their outings.

They had the best time at Halloween. The buildup was huge. They went all out on decorations. The costume decision was weeks in the planning. Faith thought back to all her costumes. Even though they could never afford a store-bought costume, her mom was always able to recreate the fashion trend of the season. Faith found a smile as she realized that all those home-made costumes were so much better than all those costumes on the store shelves she thought she needed. Faith remembered how much fun Halloween was when it occurred on a weekday. She and her friends could do nothing but plan for the evening. She couldn't remember if they even did school work, but they must have stayed busy with something because the day seemed to fly by. Halloween on the weekend was terrible. The waiting and anticipation seemed to make the day twice as long. When the time for trick-or-treating finally arrived, there was no time to waste. The route was preplanned, and timing was everything. Since candy was hard to come by when she was a kid, it was total commitment to the task at hand. Faith and her friends would gather just before dusk, and once the sun hit the horizon, they were off in search of bounty.

Inventorying the haul at the end of the evening was the highlight of weeks of anticipation. Brenda always participated in the process. She would cull out anything suspicious, but Faith always believed that she set aside all the stuff she liked. The reward and excitement of the last few weeks always overcame the spooky nature of the night, and by the end of the evening, exhaustion set in and Faith had no problem falling asleep. Remembering back, she could not recall if she ever actually made it to her bedroom, but she always woke up the next morning in her bed.

Chapter 5:
The Cookie Tin

"Faith. Faith. It's time to get up. Faith, it's time to wake up."

She slowly woke up at the beckoning of her mom's voice. It took Faith a minute to realize she was at the hospital and not in her bed at home post-Halloween. "Sorry, Mom. I must have fallen asleep. How are you feeling today?"

Brenda tried to gather her thoughts. "Faith, where are we? Am I back in the hospital? What happened? Have I been here very long?"

Faith cleared her head and attempted to straighten her hair. "We had to rush you to the hospital yesterday. You were having a seizure. The emergency room doctor told me it is likely related to the tumor. He said that Dr. Suresh will be in this morning, and they will probably run some more tests. Are you feeling OK this morning?"

Faith waited for a response, but her mom only responded with tears. Faith got up on the side of the bed and sat there holding her mom. They both cried, and cried some more, and some more, neither saying a word.

Brenda was the first to break the emotional cloud hanging over them. "Faith, I promised myself I would not waste what time I have remaining with self-pity. Can you hand me a tissue?" Brenda took the tissue, and the moment, to wipe away her sadness. Brenda spotted the cookie tin across the room. "OK, I'm better. It's all a part of God's plan. Now, so as not to leave everything up to the good Lord, can you hand me that cookie tin that you bought from the house?"

Faith walked over and picked it up and brought it back to the hospital bed, then retook her seat on the side of the bed. "Mom, what's so special about this cookie tin?" Faith looked into her mom's eyes,

The Cookie Tin

and for the first time in many weeks, she saw a real brightness.

Brenda stared at the tin for a moment before she spoke. "I hope you will forgive me for what I'm about to tell you. I have kept many things from you, and just flat lied in some cases. I have waited so long to tell you what's in this tin, but I feared it might drive you away. The way I see it now, it doesn't really matter."

"Don't talk like that, Mom. I can't imagine anything that would be in an old cookie tin that I could not forgive you for. Open it up and show me what's inside."

Brenda covered the top with her hand before speaking. "I pray that you will not hold this against me. I'm afraid you will, but first let me explain why the contents have been hidden from you for so many years. Perhaps then you will see fit to absolve me for my decisions. I never really told you why I had a rocky relationship with my parents. I regret that you missed out on the love and caring that grandparents represent, but they were far away, and seeing them only reminded me of the things in this tin, and what might have been. I let their fear and mistrust lead me astray from, perhaps, what was right. What was right was you, Faith. Because of you I was determined to move forward, and beyond my parents' fatalistic outlook."

"Back when I was younger, things were different than they are now. There was no denying, back then, that prejudice did exist, and it wasn't just exclusive to white folks. We had our own prejudices. The country, at the time, was beginning to overcome those things, but the fear and hurt still existed."

"The best summer of my life, outside of all the summers I have spent with you, was a family vacation my parents and I took," Brenda said with a smile. "It would be my last vacation with them. It was the summer we went to New Mexico. My parents and I spent several weeks there. It was a wonderful time for many reasons. The area we stayed in was small and comfortable, with a great mix of locals and tourists. It made for quiet nights and active days. We spent many days in town participating in community activities and shopping, or we would make our

The Cookie Tin

own adventures outside of town. The area offered lots of room to explore and get away. You never knew what was around the next corner or the next hill. We saw chipmunks, squirrels, elk, plenty of deer, and occasionally we caught a glimpse of a bear.

"You always had to have an umbrella in the afternoon. An afternoon shower could be counted on just as sure as the sun rose in the morning and set in the evening. I'll never forget how those afternoon showers cleaned the air and bought out the smell of the pines. You've never seen aspen as they were meant to be seen unless you've seen their leaves blowing in the rain while the sun shines through them. It's like seeing a tree full of butterflies flapping their wings.

"There were so many trees that you could not take a photo in the area without seeing hundreds. As much as I loved that area, it's not the only reason that summer visit was special." Brenda had all but forgotten her current predicament as she relived those moments.

Faith took note of how happy her mom became the more she talked about that summer. She had so many stories to share. Faith interrupted, "Did you meet anybody special?"

"I did. I met a boy. We just clicked. We were so into each other. We were inseparable for the next several weeks. We enjoyed every minute we had together. We had so many adventures with each other."

Faith could not contain her curiosity. "What was his name? What did you guys do?"

Brenda took her hand off the cookie tin just long enough to place it on Faith's hand before she continued. "In good time, but I need to tell you more.

My summer vacation was coming to an end, and so we decided to take one last hike together. It was just him and me. None of our friends this time. We had gotten deep into the forest on a trail that followed a beautiful clear gurgling stream. It was a charming setting. Then it began to rain, and it started raining hard, and as if it was meant to be, an abandoned cabin was just ahead on our path. The cabin had seen better days, but it had two important attributes. A roof and

The Cookie Tin

a fireplace with just enough scrap wood to start a fire. In no time we had a roaring fire.

"While Flash, that was his nickname, was out gathering more wood. I took off my wet clothes so they could dry in front of the fire. Let me tell you all those movies that glamorize a woman, a man, a drenching rainstorm and a shelter; it is a combination that stirs emotions within you that are irresistible."

Faith found herself laughing, half embarrassed and half in disbelief at a side of her mom she never knew existed. Faith couldn't hold the question back, "So did you guys do it?" She was embarrassed that she asked her mom this question.

Brenda looked at Faith before answering, unsure of how she should answer. "Well, I can't tell my daughter that!"

"Mom! Come on!"

Brenda placed her hands on either side of Faith's face and pulled her in close. Their eyes connected as only a mother and daughter can. "Well, where do you think you came from?"

Faith was overcome with emotion and buried her head on Brenda's shoulder.

She held that embrace until she could gather herself. "Mom, you never told me much about my father. This makes me feel so, so proud, and complete. Just to know a little about my dad. I wish I had gotten to know him before he passed. You never told me a lot about him. I always wish you had more to share about him when I was growing up."

Brenda looked down. She couldn't look Faith in the eyes. She began telling Faith about the departure and having to leave her true love and head back home. "A few weeks passed, and I realized I was pregnant. I didn't know what to do. I didn't know how to tell my parents. I didn't know how they would react. I was afraid of how they would react. However, being pregnant made me proud. It gave my life meaning and purpose. You inspired me from day one. You, growing inside of me, made me brave and resolute. I marched in one evening before we sat down for dinner, stood in front of both my mom and dad, and made the announcement.

"At first, they were shocked and stunned to the point of speechlessness. Then they went into freak out mode. 'When did this happen? What about your plans for college? Who's going to take care of this baby? And what about the dad? Who is the dad?'

"This was probably the last moment of sanity they had. As it turns out my fears and concerns were justified. When they learned who your dad was, all rationale went out the window. You see Faith, what I left out to this point is the fact that your dad was white. When my mom and dad learned this, all those years of prejudice they saw first-hand came flooding back. It clouded their reasoning. They wanted me to get an abortion. They were concerned that they, and I, would be ridiculed and humiliated and that the child would suffer the same fate. I would have no part of that and became enraged at the suggestion. Then they told me they would have no part of me or my baby."

"I told them that I knew Flash would be happy, and I was sure he would marry me, which set them off again. They went off on another insulting tirade. They told me there was no way a white boy would marry a Black girl. They said there was no way his parents would ever welcome me or my baby into their home. Worse, they said his parents would make an implausible case for how the pregnancy came to be.

"The thought of losing you sent me into a panic. I left my home that night, never to return. The fear my parents planted in me drove my decisions. I have spent many years after you were born, fearing that somebody would come and take you from me. I want you to know this before I open this tin. I want you to know what drove me to skip what might have been a wonderful and fulfilling marriage. I regret making you pay for my own fears by hiding this from you and having you miss a relationship with your father."

Brenda began crying. "My days are numbered. I hate to leave you by yourself. I don't want you grieving over my departure, although I know it is inevitable. I want you to move on. I want you to take this cookie tin and start an adventure. You see, I do not know for a fact that your dad is dead. He may still be alive. I have never tried to go back and find him. I got busy raising and loving you and never felt the need."

The Cookie Tin

With that, Brenda opened the tin. She once again looked into Faith's eyes. "Inside I have several thousand dollars, I have a senior photo of Flash, and his class ring. The name of his high school is engraved on the ring. Go! Go find him! If he is still alive, tell him how much he meant to me and how I thought of him all my life. Go find your dad!"

Chapter 6:
Moving On

Faith found herself sitting at the kitchen table where she and her mom had sat just a few weeks ago. The funeral was now past. The cookie tin sat in front of her in the middle of the kitchen table as if it were a centerpiece. Once again it captured her attention, and she was transfixed, as she had been many times the last few weeks.

Faith thought about what her mom had said. The thought of finding out about her father was exciting. What if he was still alive? That would be amazing. She did, however, have many of the same fears that her mom's parents had pushed that had destroyed her mom's ambition to seek out her first love.

Moving On

If he was alive, would he deny her existence? Would he deny the relationship with her mom ever occurring? The scenario she feared the most was that he would not even remember that day at the abandoned cabin—or even more heartbreaking, he would not remember her mom at all. That outcome made her tear up. Not only would it be a rejection of her, but a rejection of her mom's lifelong love for him, which she took to the grave.

She was entranced by the cookie tin. It produced so many tangents of thought that she could scarcely finish one before the next started. So engulfed was she, that she never heard the phone ringing until the answering machine picked up. She heard George on the other end and quickly picked up the receiver. "Hello?" Faith had not talked to him since the funeral. He had been busy with the campaign. She had been busy working through her mother's affairs.

"Faith?" George said. "I'm calling to check on you. How are you doing?"

"I'm fine, George. How are you?"

"I'm fine. I want you to get out of the house. I want you to go with me to my campaign stop tomorrow. We can go out afterward and get dinner. I want you to think about other things for a day."

Faith thought for a moment. She hadn't heard from George for a week, which made her mad, but at the same time she was ready for a break. "OK, George. What time will you be picking me up?"

George was there the next morning. He was on time today. They sped off to one of three stops for the day. The crowds were a little lighter than usual. Faith could see it was weighing on George, but he kept to his message. Faith thought his speeches would only be about five minutes long, if it weren't for the pomp and circumstance. He also had to address his competitor, labeling him as a lowlife who only carried about money and big corporations.

She thought this day would distract her from thinking about her mother, but it didn't. Faith had come to realize that those memories would always be there. She knew that one day her memories would elicit good feelings and smiles, but for now they just reminded her of the loss.

She and George were finally back in the car. They had just completed the last stop of the day. "Let's go eat," he said.

Faith was happy to hear that announcement. "I thought you would never ask."

George insisted on ordering for her, even choosing her drink. "George, I don't want to drink tonight. I'll be the driver since you have already had a couple."

"Nonsense," George said. "Drink up! If we overdo it, we can get a taxi."

Faith had a few sips of her wine but stopped at that. George kept having the waiter top of the glass. The only reason it needed topping off was because when George had finished his drink, he worked on hers until the next round arrived. George was going on and on about the campaign and all the big money that was funneling in from corporate donors. The drinking and the hypocrisy of the whole situation was off-putting.

Faith tried to discreetly inform the waiter to quit bringing drinks and to bring the bill.

George insisted on more. As usual, it turned into Faith trying to control him, but he said that he was a big boy, that he could decide when enough was enough, and that she had no right telling him what to do. She was finally able to get him out of the restaurant and into the car.

She helped George into his house and to the couch.

He wasn't content to stay on the couch, so he walked over to Faith, who was now seated at the dining table. He began blaming her for the poor crowds that day. "You have cost me my momentum. I was doing great until your mom got sick and you abandoned my campaign."

Faith was losing her patience with him. "George, you are doing fine. I'm sure it will get better the closer it gets to the election."

George put his hand on the table and leaned in towards her. "Look at all the things I do for you, and this is how you repay me?"

Faith was done at that point. "George, I'm leaving. You are not thinking straight. I'm going to take your car."

"No," he said. "You're going to sit here and tell me what you think."

"I don't think that is a good idea."

She tried to stand up, but he pushed her back down in the chair.

Faith was done. "Do not touch me! You know what's wrong with your campaign? You label your opponent as a corporate crony, while you accept their money. All the while you're out there promising government handouts for this, and handouts for that. The hope you lay at the feet of your constituents is barely enough for survival. But they wait. They wait, thinking it will get better. They wait until the next election. This election will be different—this candidate will be different. This time we will get more help. Two years turns into four years, four years into ten years, and before they know it, their kids are grown and start their own cycle. I know what a struggle it is. I lived it. I grew up with many that settled for that empty rainbow of gold. They never moved forward. Why? Because there was nothing for them to move towards. What they need is hope! Not hope for the next government handout—hope of a future. They need opportunity! They need a future! What they don't need is competition from imported cheap labor. It takes away job opportunities and any hope of a decent wage. The way things have been done in the past fosters hopelessness, bitterness, and resentment."

George slapped her across the face. Faith was stunned.

"I'm going to bed," George said as he shuffled and stumbled towards the hallway.

Faith was still stunned. She sat there at the table with her hand covering her cheek, which was still burning fiery hot. She remembered what her mom had said about George many times: "*I don't like his character.*" Faith had always given George the benefit of the doubt because he'd seemed like a good guy, but when he drank that all changed. One thing she knew from her upbringing is that life is hard. It will get complicated. She thought about the stress of the campaign and about George drinking more and more to compensate. She knew that this was just a small hurdle. *If this is how he copes now, what will it be like when a real shit storm hits?* He had never hit her before, but she decided she wasn't going to stick around and let it happen again. She grabbed a pad and pen by the phone and took it to the kitchen table. She wasn't sure what George would remember in the morning, so she left him a note. She let him know she needed time to think and to deal with the loss of her mother. She let him know she would be taking his car to her house. She would put it in the garage and leave the keys on the floorboard.

George had the code to open the garage. He could pick up the car later. She couldn't see herself continuing this relationship, so in her final sentence before signing her name, she wrote, "I really don't think our relationship will work, but I have enjoyed our friendship."

*

The next morning, George dragged himself into the kitchen. Memories from last night were slowly seeping back into his head. What he was not expecting, however, was the note she had left. He was furious. He ripped the note from the pad and threw it in the trash.

The more he thought about her breaking it off, the more furious he became. He got so mad that he thought exacting some sort of revenge was what he needed to do.

"911, what's your emergency?"

"My car has been stolen."

The police knocked on George's door. "We are here to write up a stolen vehicle. Are you George?"

"Yes, come in, officers. Thanks for coming."

"This is Officer Riley. She will be assisting me today. I'm Officer Smith."

George gave his statement, saying that he felt an acquaintance had taken his car last night without permission.

The officers looked at each other. They had dealt with this kind of issue before. "Are you sure you want to proceed with this? Don't you think you should try and get a hold of this acquaintance and resolve this without our help?"

George, still incensed, replied, "No, I would like to press charges."

Office Riley took note of the pen and pad on the kitchen table. "Can I borrow that pad for a minute?" she asked George.

Moving On

"Sure, no problem." George walked over and grabbed it and passed it to the officer.

She took the pad and then asked George if he had been writing on it today.

"No, why would you ask?"

Well, most of the time these items are found by the phone," said Officer Riley. "It looks as if somebody might have taken it to the table to leave a note. Like maybe a note about borrowing your car."

George felt his face turning red. Flush with embarrassment, he stammered with his response, "No I didn't find a note."

"Well we could take this in and run some tests and see what the last thing written on it was, but I think I can make it out without testing." She tossed the pad in front of George. "Can you read it?" she asked.

George took the pad and acted like he was struggling to make out the indentations of the writing, all the while contemplating the pickle he was now in. "Well, let me see, it does look like a note," he said. He did not want to get into too many details, so he skipped over the personal stuff and just translated what he needed to get himself out of the hole he had dug. "It looks like it says she took my car to her house and left it in the garage. Well, mystery solved," George said sheepishly. "I apologize for wasting your time today, but without your insight, Officer Riley, I might have made a big mistake."

Officer Smith jumped into the conversation. "Well, I guess our job is done here. Glad we could help."

George let them out the front door.

The officers waited till the door shut behind them, then looked at each other and rolled their eyes. "Oh brother, the crap we deal with. Riley, how did you know?"

"I didn't. It was a wild guess," she said. They laughed again as they got in the patrol car.

Chapter 7:
Keith Wells

"Keiko! Come here, girl! Where you at?" Keith said. The lab was his only partner, not to mention his savior. Keith knew something was up; she typically did not disappear for very long. She usually didn't venture off too far, as she was getting older and less prone to exploration, especially on a night like this, cold and windy, with a fresh foot of snow on the ground. It was the first storm of the season. It kept most people inside, but Keith was outside.

"Keiko! Come here, girl!" *Who wants to suffer through these conditions,* Keith thought. The wind was blowing so hard that you could barely hear what was right next to you, so he decided to waste no more energy yelling for her. He decided to give her a few more minutes before working himself up to a high level of concern. *I sure hope she shows up, otherwise I will have to get out in this mess myself.* He could not afford to lose her.

Keith went back inside to finish up the dishes. Not a big project . . . a plate, a bowl, a few pots and pans, and of course Keiko's bowl. They always ate together, their routine for almost 12 years. He'd gotten Keiko as a puppy. Or rather he'd got the dog for his daughter. His daughter had been 5 at the time. She had been asking for a dog from Santa for two Christmases. Some moments in life that are so special that the memory surfaces often. This was one of the happy ones. Giving his daughter what she longed for.

They were around the Christmas tree, on Christmas Eve, Keith with his video camera and his daughter with one of her Christmas gifts. A box with heft. He knew she had no clue what was in that box. She probably thought it contained the typical: doll, books, or a push toy. His daughter's emotional response touched both he and his wife. Keith would soon realize this moment would be a feature memory. It was a moment of pure elation, excitement, and joy wrapped into a few short minutes. He and his wife would share this memory many times that year. First laughing and then shedding a tear. It's the kind of memory that continually plays throughout a lifetime.

Keiko was a great puppy. She was playful but not rowdy. Protective without overdoing it. She barked, but not incessantly, loved to run, but not too far, and like all dogs, she loved to use her teeth, but only on her toys. Keith had found a princess. They had a big place, so a bigger dog fit well with the country surrounding their home. Keith realized what a blessing she was, thus he suggested the name Keiko, which is the Japanese word for blessing. The name stuck.

Keiko wasn't their only blessing. Their daughter was beautiful: long flowing dark hair, olive skin, big dark eyes, and a personality to match, which endeared her to any passerby. She and the dog spent a lot of time together, exploring the countryside.

His daughter loved adventure, even as a 5-year-old. Keith recalled her big adventures, within earshot and only just beyond eyesight of the house. She thought of herself as so brave, but only brave enough for her home to be just over the hill or just around the corner. Keith and his wife loved her spirit but would not dare let her know, for she might have ended up in town.

They often wondered, as most parents do, if they were making the right decisions about her upbringing. Is that kind of freedom good for a child? They had little doubt that it was a better decision than the television and video games that raise many children. They thought about their good fortune to have the space and peaceful surroundings that surrounded their home.

Every now and then they were reassured about her upbringing. Keith recalled finding his daughter in the driveway one day, after a big rainstorm. It looked like she was picking up pebbles on the driveway and moving them to the grass. "Hey, beautiful, what are you doing?"

"I'm helping," she replied.

"Sweetie, we need the rocks to stay on the driveway."

Without pausing or looking up, she said, "I'm not moving rocks, Dad, I'm moving these worms." She was picking up earthworms that had washed up among the rocks, and one by one she placed them in the grass.

"Why on earth are you doing that?" Keith asked.

"Daddy, these worms dry up if they don't get back to their home."

"Yes, but there are thousands of them."

"I know, but this one is happy." She held it up for Keith to see as it squirmed its way around her fingers. "And so are the others that I moved back to their home, before him."

"Yes, my dear. You are correct. You're such a sweetheart."

Like mother like daughter; she's a lot like her mom, Keith thought.

Keith was brought back to the present by the flip flop-flip flop of the doggy door as Keiko returned from her adventure in the winter wonderland outside. Keith was relieved! She was back, and he was dismissed from his own adventure into the blizzard on this night. Keith had dried and returned all the dishes to their proper place and was in the middle of cleaning the table when something caught his eye. Keiko had something in her mouth. It did not appear to be any of her chew toys, but it didn't immediately register with him. Keith grabbed the towel from the table and took a second look at Keiko. The object was out of place. Although Keith was across the room from Keiko, he could not look away from the object. The longer he looked, the more curious he became. When he realized what Keiko was holding, Keith's thoughts went from, *That's not what I think it is*, to *It sure looks like*, to *Where did she find that?*, to *This could be bad* in a split second.

As he approached Keiko, he tried convincing himself that the object was not what it appeared to be. It surely was something else, for if it was what he thought, it would be severely out of place, in his house, on his property, and on a night like this.

Keith's heart began racing. "Keiko, what you got there, old girl?"

He approached with caution, so as not

to incite a game of keep away. They often played fetch, but 90 percent of her fun was not giving up her prized toy. Much to his relief, she gave up her prize quickly, and just as quickly Keith's concern was confirmed.

Keiko was in possession of a small billfold; it appeared to be a lady's. It was somewhat wet and cold from the weather outside. Keith's mind raced through the probabilities and came to one conclusion. On a night like this, Keiko likely did not dig this up, and if it was found lying about, its owner could be in trouble. Keith wasted no further time. He had to assume the worst, for on a night like this, he couldn't rule out the grave possibility that someone was stranded in the elements. He would have to go outside.

Keith had avoided the search for Keiko in the bad weather, but now he was on a much bigger search. He was hoping it was nothing, but his imagination was running wild. He had to prepare. The last thing he wanted to do was get out there and find that he didn't have what he needed. He was committing to one trip out, and a full investment to ease his mind of all possible scenarios. He didn't want to look back tomorrow and regret not trying. Like most of his actions in life, he didn't want to rest until he felt he had done everything he could.

Keith grabbed his coat, donned his snow boots, and headed out with his best flashlight. He shut the doggy door before leaving. He left Keiko barking as he closed the door behind him. He made it down the front steps when he looked out upon the gravity of the task at hand. It was not the cold that frightened him; he was dressed to handle that. It was the heavy snowfall. The snow was propelled by high winds. He was amazed at how white it was. It was the opposite of the darkest nights out here. He switched on the flashlight, but unlike its piercing capabilities on dark nights, it barely allowed visibility to exceed five feet beyond where he stood. As he trudged through the snow, he regretted not owning a pair of snowshoes, but snowfalls like this were rare. And when they occurred, Keith stayed inside until the snow subsided enough for him to venture outside.

Keith stopped. He began patting his pants pocket, then moved to his coat pocket.

He had forgotten his phone. If he got too far from the house and needed it, it would be more wasted time if someone were in trouble. He trudged back to the house, stepping in the footprints he had just made. He blasted through the door, grabbed his phone, and headed toward the door again. Keiko was there looking at him, using the wishful expression she used when she wanted out. Keith stopped for only a second. "Not now, girl."

He made it off the steps, once again, and took a quick look back at the house. He was glad he had turned on all the floodlights before he ventured outside. If nothing else, they would provide a glow that he hoped to depend on for his safe return. As he looked back, he was glad to see his footprints in the snow. This would help, but they would not survive long before being covered up and gone forever, lost to the wind and the many thousand snowflakes. He had no longer finished the thought when his mind found a foothold on the situation. *Keiko must have left a path! If I hurry, I can locate that before it is buried and retrace her steps.* Then another epiphany: *What if she could lead me to where she found the wallet?*

Keith moved as quickly as he could back to the house, where Keiko had started barking again. *Could we be on the same page here? Is she trying to tell me she can help*? He needed help. He needed a clue to the direction he would take. As he opened the door, she came out just like it was any other day when she could escape the confines of the house and be outside. Without hesitation, she made her way down the steps and took a right. She had just made it to the edge of the house and what would be the driveway, if not for the snow. When she made a turn down the driveway, Keith's spotlight was able to pick up a faint path that she undoubtedly had made upon her earlier return. Keith followed her and the path and found some sense of direction. It appeared she had come up the lane that led to their driveway.

Keiko and Keith made their way down the lane. Keiko's earlier path became much clearer as Keith entered the portion of the lane covered by trees. Keith's progress improved greatly because of the wind break and added protection of the branches overhead. This was a great place during the summer for evening walks. He and his wife loved to take this route after the sun was setting and the air began to cool. Few visitors ventured up this lane, so it was always peaceful. If a car drove there, it was either lost or coming to his house.

Keith's pace picked up. The snow was not drifting or quite as deep under the trees, and his flashlight was now exceeding its earlier limitations. It appeared as if Keiko's path was heading towards the road. Although the lane was less than a quarter mile from its connection with the road, their trip tonight would take much longer. The spotlight finally picked up what appeared to be the end of the lane. It was eerie. It was like viewing the end of a tunnel, which tonight ended at a solid white wall. Just as Keith spotted the end of the road, Keiko took off, barking and running straight for the main road. Keith tried to keep up, but his two feet were no match for her four. He could tell she had stopped, as her barking seemed to be stationary.

Keith approached the white wall of blowing snow, where visibility again decreased and the snow depth increased. He could still hear Keiko barking. She was still stationary. Keith finally sighted Keiko and a large dark shadow just in front of her. He could not make it out, but there was something there. The shape didn't compute. Keith made it only a few steps farther when his mind deciphered the shape and the gravity of the situation. It was a car, and it was upside down. "This is not good," he told himself, beginning to run.

He had no idea what he would find but made haste towards the car. As he approached, Keiko's barking continued, which hindered his ability to hear any noise or movement from the car. "Good girl, Keiko. Good girl." She settled down, as Keith began digging snow from around the driver's door.

It was at this moment that Keith realized how important his return trips to the house were. He had his phone and Keiko had taken him right to the car.

Keith grabbed his light, and it immediately picked up what looked like long dark hair. There was a little blood that had dripped down on the snow on the inside roof of the car. Keith was hoping the small amount of blood would be good news. He called inside. "Are you OK? Can you hear me?" The driver gave no response. Keith realized he could not get to the victim from the driver's door. He made his way to the passenger side. Keith kept his gloves on as he crawled inside the window There was a lot of glass. He was trying to orient himself before removing his gloves so he could check for a pulse. Finally situated, he took his gloves off. He was somewhat relieved to find the driver was still warm. He quickly grabbed his phone and dialed 911. He put the phone on speaker and laid it down so he could get a better idea of the driver's condition.

"Hello, this is 911, what's your emergency?"

"A car has flipped, and the driver is hanging upside down, still in their seat belt."

"Were you involved in the wreck?" asked the operator."

"No, I just found the wreck."

"Sir, what's the condition of the accident victim?"

"They are unconscious!"

"Can you find a pulse?"

"They are still warm, but I'm not sure."

"Can you provide your location?"

"Yes!" Keith stammered as he tried to provide the location. A normally easy question becomes very difficult when your adrenaline is racing through your body and the location is not an address. "Yes, I'm off of . . . I'm off of 156."

"Where exactly?" asked the operator.

"Let me give you my home address. You can find the wreck on your way to my house. I'm at 3300 Pine Valley Road."

"Thank you, sir. I have emergency personnel on their way."

Keith was relieved to have someone on the other end of the line, even if they weren't there to help.

"Now let's focus on the victim, or victims, sir. Are there any other passengers?"

That question elevated Keith's anxiety to a new level. "I have no idea!"

"Sir, can you tell me what you see in the car and around the car?"

Keith frantically used his flashlight and quickly scanned the inside of the car. "I don't see any other passengers."

"What do you see, sir?"

"I see a suitcase, a hanging bag, a coat. That's all I see."

"OK, it sounds like we are dealing with one person, but can you scan the area around the car for any other potential victims?"

"I'm leaving my phone inside the car, ma'am. I'll take a quick look around."

He put his gloves back on and crawled back out the passenger side and took a quick look around. Nothing. The path of the wreck itself didn't give any indication that somebody might have been thrown from the car, much to his relief. The snow seemed undisturbed, and Keith was praying that Keiko, who was now lying patiently in the snow, would be aware if any other victims were outside the car.

Keith crawled back in through the window. "I don't see any other passengers."

"OK, sir, now let's focus on the victim. Are they still unconscious?"

"Yes, they are still not responding."

"How long has the victim been hanging upside down?"

"I have no clue."

"Is the victim's skin cold or warm?"

"It's warm."

"Are they male or female? Are there any signs of trauma?"

"There is a small amount of blood, but I can't tell where it is coming from."

"Sir, is it pooling?"

"Is what pooling?"

"The blood. Is it pooling?"

"It's hard to tell; it could be soaking through the snow."

"Sir, we would normally not have you move the victim, but with a victim bleeding, head hanging down, length of time since the accident unknown, the weather conditions, which will also impede our response time, I say we get them out of that seatbelt. Can you help us with that?"

Keith tried to position himself underneath the victim. It was not going to be easy.

He crawled farther into the vehicle and braced himself against the dashboard. This left just enough room for the victim to be positioned just over his lap. It also provided direct access to the button for the seatbelt. Keith caught his breath, "OK, I think I can get them out now."

"OK, sir, do the best that you can to support the victim as you release the seatbelt. We want you to minimize the movement of the neck and back as you release the belt."

Keith repositioned himself so that he could use his back and shoulders to support the victim and pushed the button for the seat belt. It all happened rather quickly, but the victim came loose and ended up in his lap. "It's a female," Keith stated. "The victim, it's a lady."

"Sir, you have done a wonderful job. Can you find that coat you mentioned earlier, and put it over her?"

"Sure." Keith found the coat and placed it over her. It was now a waiting game. He was now all in on saving this girl, but all he had to comfort her were his words, "I've got you;

everything will be OK. Hang in there; help is on its way. I have you! I have you! I'm not leaving! I'm not leaving!"

Chapter 8:
Wells Mill and Lumber

"Mr. Wells, thank you again. It's not every day that you get to save somebody's life." The paramedics had loaded the lady into the ambulance and were preparing to leave. "Will you be OK, to get back to your house?"

"Sure thing. You guys take it easy on your way to the hospital." They were off as Keith turned back up the lane leading to his house. It was only then that Keith was once again conscious of the frigid cold and heavy snowfall. He had been outside for over an hour and had not once thought of the snow or the cold. Keith made his way home with Keiko by his side; he had to apologize to her. "They said I saved that lady's life, Keiko, but the credit should go to you." Keith often talked to Keiko. She always looked at him when he talked to her, just like she was taking in every word.

They made it back to the front porch. Keith grabbed a broom and began sweeping off the front steps, and the path leading to the door. He swept his boots and shook off his coat, and now it was Keiko's turn. Keith ran his hand wildly through Keiko's fur. She loved being petted, no matter how aggressively. Keith set the broom aside and stopped for a moment to take in the night. The wind had slowed, although the snow showed no signs of letting up.

As a kid, these were the exact conditions that he loved. Even though he grew up some ways from the train tracks, the sound of the train's horn seemed to ride on every snowflake on nights like this. It was always the only sound one could hear, other than that of the rhythmic *click, click* of the snowflakes. It was so peaceful that he would totally fixate on the train as it slowly receded into the night. It transfixed him until the sound had completely vanished.

Wells Mill and Lumber

There were no trains out here, but that wasn't a bad thing.

"Let's head inside, Keiko." They made their way back in and welcomed the conditions inside: no wind, no snow, and a balmy 67 degrees. Back in the kitchen, Keith finished up the dishes and remembered the object that started this evening's events. The billfold still sat on the table. Although he felt the need to rush the personal belongings of the victim to the hospital, he thought better, due to the weather and the lack of importance of the belongings would have tonight. He decided it would be best to call the hospital. The hospital took his name and number and said they would get back in touch.

Tomorrow was a big day. It was only last week that he had met with the Dundy Corporation. They had made a very generous offer for his business. He stood to make a lot of money and meander his way to a leisurely retirement.

Wells Mill and Lumber Yard was the result of many hard years of work by his dad. Keith now carried on the tradition and legacy his father left him 18 years ago. His dad had left him rather abruptly at the age of 60 due to cancer. Keith was 32 when he took over. He had learned a lot from his dad, but ready or not, the business was his without choice.

Keith and his dad didn't talk a lot of shop back in those days. They put in a good days' work and left it there till the next day. Keith recalled the exact day he found out that his dad was sick. Keith saw him walk into the office, and he could see something was not right.

It's hard to hide the shock of news like that. His dad was no better at that than anyone else, when one learns that their days are numbered. Your posture, your gate, the look on your face—it's like a dark cloud. It was especially evident that day on his dad, who was normally an upbeat and happy person. Keith had only seen that look one other time, when his mom passed.

Keith was doing inventory that day, when his dad walked in. He went right to his office. Keith recalled following him right in. "Dad, what's wrong?"

The first thing he said was, "Damn, I stink at hiding things! Either that or you're just like your mother. She could tell any time I was up to something. Like that day you told me you and Carli were expecting. Remember that? You guys were coming over to dinner that night to make the big announcement. Of course, you had already told me. When I walked into the house that night, she was all over me. I couldn't hide it and I couldn't hold the news."

"Dad, you are not hiding good news. I can see it written all over you."

He paused and looked down for a long time. "My sun is setting. I'm sick. I have stinking cancer. I don't have long."

Keith could still recall the sick feeling of that day. It started in his stomach and worked its way up to his head, ending there in disbelief. Questions started pouring out, "Are you sure? How do you know? When did you find out? Can we fight this? How long do you have? What are we going to do?" His dad's news settled into the pit of his stomach and welled up in his throat like a ball of cotton. Keith tried to speak, but he knew trying to speak one word would have allowed his emotions to overflow and pour out like the downpour of rain in a thunderstorm. He didn't want his dad to see that.

For several minutes, they both sat there with their heads down, both overcome by the unbearable reality of the situation. Then they both got up and hugged. Keith recalled holding on, as if letting go would separate them forever. "Dad, I don't want to let you go."

"I know son. This sucks. I'm really going to miss all of this . . . my family, my work."

That last sentence stuck with Keith. To this day it was hard to remember those words without his throat balling up and tears just appearing as if a switch had been turned on. It always made him sad to think of the finality of his dad's passing. At the time, it made Keith even more emotional to think of all the people his dad had to say goodbye to. *For me and others it was him leaving us, but for him, he had to leave everybody behind. He loved us, he loved his work, but he loved his work because of the people who made it successful.*

Wells Mill and Lumber

The employees were like his second family. He treated them very well. This was the one thing that Keith had tried his best to keep alive once he took over the business.

Keith was ready to turn in, but the adrenaline still percolated through his body. He could not stop thinking of the accident, the poor lady in the car, and all the questions surrounding that. He also had the presentation he had prepared for the employees the next morning cycling repeatedly through his head.

Keiko sensed it also. She got up beside Keith on the couch and curled up. What good therapists dogs are. Keith started petting her, and the next thing he knew his phone alarm was going off.

It took him a minute to realize he had fallen asleep on the couch; regardless, he still felt pretty good. The billfold sitting on the table shook the notion that last night had been just a nightmare.

Keith always hit the thermostat, the very first thing, and started a pot of coffee. It was chilly, and warming himself, and the house, was priority number one. There would be no need for him to rush out the door this morning. It would probably be after nine o'clock before the plows hit the highway in his area. They never made it up his lane, or his driveway, but his truck had a plow on it. It would get him down the driveway and the lane until he reached the highway.

"Keiko, let's get you outside." Keith opened the door to a winter wonderland. It had probably snowed close to two feet. He could see the clouds thinning out, the wind had died down, and the sun would soon be making an appearance. It would shine on the front porch and quickly warm things up. Keiko would stay out this morning, and so would Keith. He bundled up and took his coffee on the porch. A beautiful ending to the ferocious weather of last night.

Keith thought it best to call the hospital before he headed out. After working through several layers of transfers, he finally was able to find somebody to help him.

"Mr. Wells, thanks for calling. I understand you have our patient's belongings?"

"Yes, I do."

"She is doing very well. We are trying to locate her family. Mr. Wells, don't rush that purse in this morning, just drop it off later when the roads clear up."

"Who should I ask for?" asked Keith.

"Ask for Alice."

Keith finally made it into work. Two seconds in, two steps through the entrance was all it took for the bantering to start. "About time." "Are we working bank hours now?" "Did you get lost on your way in?"

"Good morning to you all," Keith said. "I guess everybody survived the snowstorm?"

Events like this broke the routine and always affected the energy and activity level in the shop. "We are bringing in lunch today, so if you brought something from home, store it in the snow bank for tomorrow, or if you prefer the civilized form, put it in the fridge. This will be a working lunch." He heard some groans as he entered his office. Working lunch was definitely appreciated, but nine times out of ten it meant more safety and regulation education. This had become a routine lately, as his business, like many others, was slowly being bogged down by the muck of government oversight and regulation. Those laws and rules didn't come without a cost, to not only Wells Mill and Lumber Yard's bottom line, but also to the time taken away from work.

*

"Thanks for the pizza, Mr. Wells."

The staff was just finishing up lunch. Dan spoke up, "Keith, I thought this was going to be a working lunch?"

"It is, Dan. We are about to get started. I wanted to make sure there were no distractions for our visit today," Keith said. "We have some important things to discuss today. Why don't we get started. How about some input from the group? Anybody can answer. The more the better. What's the one thing you cherish most in your life?"

Billy was the first to jump in. He was never afraid to voice his opinion. He was also the youngest and newest staff member. "My mom," he said. The group chuckled.

Charlie jumped at the chance to add his comment. "Billy, you really need to find a

Wells Mill and Lumber

girl, but you better make sure she will pick up your dirty socks and underwear." The group burst out in laughter.

"I'm working on it, Charlie. Your daughter and I are going out this weekend."

The others ooh'd at the quick comeback.

Keith decided he better jump back in. "We all love our mothers."

Dan spoke next; he had been with Wells Mill and Lumber for a while, "My wife and kids." All the others nodded in agreement.

"Anybody else?" asked Keith. "Family, without a doubt, very important to all.

"Would you say that most of you have this job to support your families?" Once again, the group nodded in agreement. "Next question, what would you do if you did not have this job? What if this company did not exist?" The group got nervous and quiet with that question. "Frank, you have been here a while. What would you do?"

Frank thought a minute before answering. "Well, if tomorrow I woke up and this job was gone, I would probably just retire. If the job was never here to begin with, I would probably be living somewhere else, or my

97

family's lifestyle would be much more limited."

"Thanks, Frank," Keith said.

Dan spoke next. "I think Frank is right—we would probably all be living somewhere else." The group agreed.

Keith decided it was time to break the news. "Eighteen years ago, my dad passed, and I took over this company. It was my dad's wish that each employee become an owner in this company, and so we set that up, that first year. As each of you know, we do not have stock, but each of you, depending on your tenure, are partial owners. The more tenure, the greater the share in ownership. I tell you this because if you decide to retire or move on into another job, then you can collect your funds upon departure. A large corporation has made a generous offer for Wells Mill and Lumber. Our more tenured employees stand to make a good bit of money and could retire, if they chose. Now, all of you will get a chance to vote, and you are free to come by the office and see what kind of money you might be able to walk away with if we do decide to sell.

Everybody, stand up. Go ahead, everybody, stand up. Now look around at your fellow employees. Think about what we just discussed because how you vote may very well decide their future, the future of their family, and the future of this community. Now, are there any questions?"

Charlie was the first to speak, "What if we do not sell?"

"Thanks, Charlie," said Keith. "Charlie asked a very important question. This is also something that each of you should keep in mind. If we do not sell, it is very likely that this corporation could go down the highway to our competitor and make the same generous offer. They might sell. If they do, it is likely they would take over our competitor and try to drive us out of business. If this happens, it is my belief that we need a backup plan. I do have some ideas in the works if that were to happen."

Keith fielded questions for several more minutes. "If there are no more questions, I'm going back to the office. I will be there for the next two hours. Feel free to drop in and inquire about what your share might be if we were to sell, or if you have more questions, I will be glad to answer them. Talk to your families tonight and we will vote tomorrow."

Keith retired to his office. He had not been at his desk long when Frank walked in.

"Have a seat, Frank," Keith suggested.

"No need. I already know I'm voting not to sell."

"Wow, I thought you may be ready to retire."

"I could, but I might drive Dacy crazy, chasing her around the house all day. Besides, I don't want to leave all these young folks and their families in a bad spot. Another thing, Keith. What you did out there, talking about families and community, considering how you lost Carli, and . . . well, anyway, I know that must have been hard, but thank you for that." Frank shook Keith's hand and turned and walked out.

Keith stood behind his desk and stared at the doorway, trying to shake the emotions that brief encounter elicited. His eyes filled with tears thinking about the things he had lost. The phone rang, which shook him out of his past. He took a minute before answering, to shake his head back and forth and clear his emotions. "Hello."

"Mr. Wells, it's Alice at the hospital. I was told you are planning on dropping our patient's billfold off today."

Yes, that's correct. Should I bring it now?"

"No, no rush. The patient wants you to drop it off in person."

Chapter 9: Recovery

Faith awoke in a strange place and with a splitting headache. The sun was shining through the window, but the window was frosty around the perimeter. That was something she had never seen. It only added to her confusion, but it did start to reload her memory bank. She remembered driving in the snow last night, but where was she and why was she driving in the snow? She began taking in her surroundings with a little better understanding. Before Faith could grasp the breadth of her situation, someone knocked on the door.

In walked a lady she did not recognize, and she was in scrubs.

Recovery

"How are you feeling?" she asked.

Faith lifted her head up off the pillow but put it back down immediately. Not only was her head hurting, but her neck was very sore. "Am I in the hospital?" Faith asked.

"You are. I'm your nurse. My name is Alice."

"How long have I been in here?"

"You came in last night."

"How did I get here . . . to the hospital?"

"You came in on an ambulance."

"Oh!" Faith took that last bit of information in, and it rolled around in her head for a few seconds. "Where are my things, and what about my car? Do you know what happened?"

"All in due time, but let's get you taken care of first." Alice began with a few questions. "Now, let's get an idea of how hard a hit your head took. What's your name?"

"My name? My name is Faith."

"Well, that's a good sign. Now, let me ask again, how are you feeling?

"My neck and head hurt. Am I OK?"

Alice didn't hesitate with her answer. "We'll let the doctor discuss that with you, but I'm thinking you are fine, considering the bump you took to your head, and besides, we are here to take good care of you. Let me call the doctor and tell him you are awake and see if we can get you something for your head and neck." With that, Alice was out the door, but not for long. She stuck her head back in. "Faith, can you lift up your left hand?"

Faith did so without hesitation.

"And your right hand?" Faith complied again. "Another good sign. Now see that cable with the large remote connected to it? It's by your right hand."

Faith lifted her head with a little more caution this time. She found the remote and held it up. "You mean this one?"

"That's right! You got it! You can push the button to call us for anything you need and use it to operate the television." With that, Alice was gone.

Faith looked out the window. She was still working on putting all the pieces back together. Outside was a winter wonderland, unlike anything she had witnessed in her 30 years. Her mind drifted away from deciphering her current predicament and focused instead on the stunning beauty outside. The trees seemed to have a fresh coat of white paint over the top of each branch. The greenery underneath the snow seemed to hold tiny white clouds. The sun was out, which not only made it a very bright day, but it reflected off the snow, which gave the snow the appearance of crystal glitter. Her gaze drifted off to the mountains that loomed in the background. They also had a fresh coat of white. The snow made everything look neat, clean, and organized.

As much as Faith wanted to take in the scenery, she had to shut her eyes. The brightness was giving her twice the headache she had awoken to. Faith's thoughts drifted back to the many days she spent with her mom in the hospital. She missed her mom and often thought of her. She knew her mom was in a better place, but the reality of having no one by her side, as she had been for her mom, really concealed the fact that she was alone. She would have no visitors, no flowers, and no one to help her once she left the hospital. The depressing reality she found herself in started tears running down her checks.

"We don't allow crying in the hospital without a good reason," came a voice from the doorway. Faith turned her head away to try and hide her tears. "And because you are alive, healthy, and on the road to recovery, you shouldn't be crying. And beautiful, even with the bandage on your head. Sorry, ignore that last part. If administration catches wind of me saying you're beautiful—well, I would hate to think of the consequences. But of course, I'm just stating the obvious. Faith, I'm Doctor Stephens."

Faith used the back of her hand to wipe the tears from her cheek before turning to face the doctor. "I'm sorry, the sunshine outside, it's making my head hurt."

"Would you like me to pull the shade down?"

"Please."

Doctor Stephens walked toward the window and kept talking as he lowered the shade. "OK, so Faith, everything looks good, but we are dealing with a head injury.

We will probably keep you for a few days. Is there anybody that you would like us to contact?"

"No, I'm fine."

"No family, husband. Boyfriend, maybe?"

"No, I'm good," Faith repeated.

"Maybe a girlfriend? Or a friend that is a girl?"

Faith laughed. "No and no, I'm straight, if that's what you were asking."

"Well, my job here is done. I have made you laugh! You are free to go! Just kidding. I can't let you go just yet. Besides, we only just met. I need time to think of more questions that are completely unrelated to your health and well-being. OK, it's your turn. What questions do you have for me?"

The distraction was good for a Faith. A little conversation does a lot to clear out the cobwebs. "Does anyone know where my things are?"

Doctor Stephens hesitated. "Hmm, I'm not sure, but we can look into that for you."

"How about my car?"

"We can look into that, too. I'm looking for questions more like, 'Will I live to see my

30th birthday?' 'Will I have a full recovery?' 'Will I always have this scar on my head?' or 'How is the food here?'"

"Scar? Do I have a scar on my head? How bad is it?" asked Faith in a bit of a panic.

"I'm glad you asked. Let's take a look." Doctor Stephens grabbed a small mirror from the table next to the bed. Faith held the mirror while he unwrapped the bandages. As the bandages came off, Doctor Stephens exclaimed, "Extraordinary, someone has done a remarkable job with these stitches. This is the work of a fine craftsman."

Faith was now warming up to the personality of Doctor Stephens. "I guess you did this work?"

"Then you have seen my work before?"

Faith laughed again. She pointed to a spot on her head just along the hairline. "If it wasn't for my head hurting right here, I wouldn't have known where to look."

Doctor Stephens smiled as they both looked at each other, not knowing where the conversation should go next.

"Well, the nurse says you need something for your head and neck pain. I will take care of that. Are there any other questions?"

"Yes, one other. How *is* the food?"

Doctor Stephens smiled. "It's not home cooking, but it's good for hospital food. I will be back to check on you. For now, just relax, maybe listen to some soft music. Keep the TV off. It will probably have the same effect as our snow-covered terrain outside."

Faith stopped Doctor Stephens before he made it out the door. "I made it."

Dr. Stephens hesitated, trying to figure out what she was talking about.

"I made it to my 30th birthday." They both smiled, and he was out the door.

Alice returned to Faith's room with medication in very short order. "OK, honey can you swallow pills?"

"Sure." Faith grabbed the cup from the swing table beside her bed.

"Faith, Doctor Stephens asked me to check on your things. It seems that your car is in bad shape. The sheriff's office sent an officer down to retrieve your belongings from your car. I also found out that Mr. Wells has your billfold. He is supposed to bring it by later today."

"Mr. Wells, who is that? How did he get my billfold?"

"We all love Mr. Wells. He is a local business owner. The story I heard is that he is the one that found and rescued you. If not for him, my dear . . . well, I hate to think what might have happened to you. You might have been out there in that freezing blizzard till dawn. I only wish someone had been there for his family way back when."

"What happened?"

"He lost his wife and only daughter to a drunk driver. It was quite the tragedy back then, but Mr. Wells has carried on. Bless his heart. That incident still haunts all of us to this day."

"That's terrible! I must thank him. Can you make sure he brings my billfold up to me? I would like to personally thank him."

"I sure will. Can I get you anything else?"

"No, I'm fine. I think I will just get some rest."

Alice went straight to the phone to call Mr. Wells.

*

Recovery

Faith was not sure how long she was out, but she awoke to the sounds of discussion in her room. Alice was talking with a young man in uniform.

"Faith, we are sorry to disturb you, but this is Billy. He is here with your belongings."

"Hey, Ms. Faith. How are you feeling?"

"I think I'm doing better."

"Glad to hear that. Where should I set your things? How about I put them over here on this chair?"

Faith took inventory from her bed. She saw her coat, hanging bag, and her suitcase, and was much relieved to know that they all appeared intact and undamaged. "Billy, can I ask you a question?"

"By all means. How can I help?" "

"Do you know what happened to me?"

Billy hesitated a moment before replying. "Well, you had a roll-over accident during the snowstorm. You ended feet up. Sorry—your wheels in the air and roof on the ground. Somehow, Mr. Wells found you. He lives quite a way off the highway. I'm not sure why he was down that direction.

It's quite a walk from his house, but anyway, here you are, safe and sound."

"Thanks, Billy. Thanks for bringing my belongings."

"I wish you a speedy recovery, and God bless, Ms. Faith." Billy exited the room.

"Alice, can you help me with my suitcase?" Alice gathered Faith's suitcase and brought it to the swing table. "I need to make sure my cookie tin is still inside. Can you open the suitcase and see if you can find it?"

Alice rummaged through clothing until she finally found the cookie tin. She took it out and handed it to Faith. "Those must be some good cookies!" exclaimed Alice.

"Oh, it's not cookies, it's the reason I'm visiting. I just wanted to make sure everything was still inside."

"Oh, so this is where you were coming. We all thought you were just passing through. Well, we are glad to have you. I wish our weather had treated you better." Alice smiled. "Do you have family here?"

Faith thought about how to answer that question. "Well, maybe. I'm trying to find someone." Faith began to open the cookie tin. "Maybe you can help?" She had barely gotten the words out when there was a light knock on the door.

"Hello!" came a voice from behind the door.

"Yes, come in," Faith said. From behind the door stepped a smartly dressed older gentleman with a peaceful face and well-kept hair.

"Hello, Mr. Wells. Come in. Meet Faith. Faith, this is Mr. Wells. I'll leave you two. I need to see to my other patients." Alice exited the room.

"So, you are Faith?" Mr. Wells asked as he extended his hand.

Faith shook his hand as she took note of the handsome man before her. "Yes," was all she could say has she continued to shake his hand.

"Well, it's nice to meet you," Keith said.

Faith realized she was still shaking his hand and quickly withdrew.

"Welcome to our little town," he added.

Faith finally realized she was still fixated on his eyes and diverted her gaze.

"I wish we had provided a warmer welcome for you."

"Thank you, Mr. Wells."

"Call me Keith, please. Mr. Wells is way too formal. How are you feeling?"

"I'm much better. Thank you for saving my life."

"Well now, that's a bit dramatic, but you were in a precarious situation. Besides, it wasn't me who found you. It was Keiko."

"Keiko?" She wanted Mr. Wells to clarify, but having heard of the family tragedy he'd suffered, she hesitated to ask.

Keith was quick to recognize that Faith was puzzled. "Keiko is my dog. She found your billfold and bought it to me. That started an adventure that I won't soon forget!" exclaimed Keith. "By the way, here is your billfold. Do you pass through here often? You look familiar." Keith knew she wasn't from his town but thought maybe she was a vacationer. Lots of people visited the area both summer and winter and frequently return.

"No, this is my first visit. I need to thank Keiko sometime."

"Yes, I think we can arrange that. She loves company. She gets bored with just me. When you get to feeling better, plan on staying a few extra days. We can show you around town. I have an arrangement with one of the lodges in town. With my business, I often have visitors in town. They can take care of you."

"Mr. Wells, I wouldn't want to—"

"Nonsense! My treat. It's the least I can do considering all you have been through. Remember it's Keith. Not Mr. Wells." Keith surveyed her room. "Is Tad taking good care of you?"

"Tad?" Faith asked, not knowing who he was speaking of.

"Tad, your doctor. Sorry, Doctor Stephens."

"Oh, yes. He stopped by this morning. He seems like a good doctor. And he's funny, too."

"Well, good. We love him around here. He takes good care of all of us. I better be going. I'll leave my number with Alice. I'll also leave the name of the lodge. They will be expecting you once you leave here.

I'm glad to see you doing so well." With that, Mr. Wells walked into the hallway to find Alice.

"Alice, do you have a minute? Has nobody sent that poor kid any flowers?"

"Mr. Wells, I don't think she has any family. Doctor Stephens and I were talking about that this morning."

"What a shame. Such a beautiful girl. If you feel she needs anything, please let me know. I told her to stay at the lodge once she leaves here. You can give her my phone number as well."

Chapter 10:
Tad Stephens

Faith lay in her bed. She was not sure if she was home or still in the hospital. She was comfortable lying there with her eyes still closed, taking in the smell of coffee, the whispering voices, and the clank of dishes. She didn't really want to wake herself up. She was so comfortable and familiar with what she was smelling and hearing. That ended when she rolled over and recognized that painful spot on her head. Then she knew she was still in the hospital. She finally gave in and opened her eyes to find her room had completely changed. Several vases held beautiful flowers. She had to sit up in bed to determine if she was still dreaming.

Every spot that had a level surface had a vase, every vase was full of flowers, and every vase had a different cluster and type of flower.

"Good morning, honey," came the familiar voice of Alice from beside her bed.

"Good morning. What happened to my room?"

"Oh, you must be referring to the flowers? Aren't they lovely? Mr. Wells sent them over this morning."

"He sent all these?" Faith asked in disbelief.

"Yes, do you have a favorite?"

"Hum, I'll have to take a closer look, but right now I'm amazed, so I would have to say all of them." Faith sat back in her bed and closed her eyes again. "How long did I sleep?"

"Did you meet Toni last night? She was on duty during the night," Alice said.

"No, I don't remember a Toni."

"Well then, you have been asleep for a very long time. You probably missed Doctor Stephens as well. He came by at the end of my shift yesterday. He sat with you a long time."

Faith still had her eyes closed, trying to warm up to the new day. "Yeah, I don't remember Doctor Stephens stopping by, either."

"Let's get you some breakfast. It will help you wake up this morning."

Alice returned a few minutes later with a tray of breakfast. She was moving things around to place the tray in a better position when Faith spoke. "Birds of paradise."

"Birds of paradise?"

"Birds of paradise. Over there." Faith pointed across the room. "Those are my favorite flowers."

"Oh, I love those, too. There, you are all set. Doctor Stephens will be in shortly," Alice added as she exited the room.

In a short amount of time, Doctor Stephens entered the room. He was preoccupied with some paperwork. Faith watched him as he walked up to the bed, never looking up or taking his eyes off the papers in hand. He hesitated at the bedside. Faith started to say something but decided against it. Finally, he looked up. "Good morning," he said, as he made eye contact. "Good Lord!" was his quick follow-up. "What happened in here? Am I at the florist?"

Faith burst out in laughter. "Can you believe it? This is what I woke up to this morning. Mr. Wells had all of these sent over."

Dr. Stephens acted like he was yelling at Alice outside the room. "Alice! Cancel that floral arrangement I ordered. There is no room." He grinned. "Well, I love them, but there is just so many. I hope you don't have allergies! How was your breakfast?"

Faith hesitated with her response. "It's good."

"I bet you're getting tired of the same old stuff. It's time you get up and about more today. How about I bring you lunch today? We have a great hamburger place in town. I'll pick up the burgers and we can eat down in the cafeteria. What do you think?"

Faith replied without hesitation. "That would be wonderful. I was just thinking about a hamburger as I choked down that sausage patty this morning." They laughed.

"Faith, you are responding very well. Why don't you go for a walk around the hospital today? Inside, not outside. If that goes well, we will get you out of here. I'll meet you in the cafeteria for lunch."

*

Lunch couldn't get here fast enough. She had been thinking about hamburgers and french fries since the conversation earlier that morning. She decided to go ahead and get up and gather herself and walk around the hospital until lunchtime arrived. Faith smiled at herself in the mirror as she combed her hair. She picked up her make-up bag and then set it back down, saying to herself, "Really? No!"

She walked out into the hallway. "Alice, I think I'm going for a walk."

"Doctor Stephens said that you might get out of your room today."

"Alice, does Doctor Stephens have any kids?"

"No kids. And not married, in case you are curious."

Although she was curious, she did not intend to be so conspicuous. "Thanks, Alice. I was just wondering."

After passing the cafeteria twice, with no sign of Doctor Stephens or the hamburgers, she headed back toward her room. She found Alice at the front desk. "Alice, can you let Doctor Stephens know I'm in the cafeteria?" With that, Faith grabbed a magazine from the waiting area and headed down the hall.

She hadn't been down there long when Doctor Stephens came in with the goods. "Wow, I almost didn't recognize you," Faith said. Doctor Stephens was out of uniform—no scrubs, no white coat.

"Well, I'm off. I took off so I could get you lunch and take you, and all your flowers, to the lodge. We are breaking you out of here today."

"I don't know which is better, getting out of here or this hamburger. Thanks for everything, Doctor Stephens."

"OK, time to call me Tad. No more Doctor Stephens. If anybody hears you call me 'Doctor' in here, then they are likely to put me back to work."

"Are you sure you don't mind dropping me off at the lodge?"

"It's not a problem. It's just down the road. How is that hamburger?"

"Really good. I might need to eat there a few more times before I leave. Is it close?"

"It's very close to the lodge, and there is a great diner nearby, as well. What brought you to town, by the way?"

Faith grabbed a few more french fries before responding. "I'm looking for a relative that I lost touch with. Are you from here?"

"My grandparents had a place here. I spent many summers here when I was younger. They have passed, but it's hard to shake the allure of this area, so I came back here to practice medicine."

"I'm still trying to figure out what I want to do. How did you get into medicine?"

"That's a good question. I think it was meant to be. You might say fate. My grandfather was a big outdoors guy. He would rather have been outside than inside, but as he got older, his heart began to give him problems, but he refused to let it slow him down. He used to always tell me, 'If you're not out living life, then you're just waiting to die.' Even when his heart was giving him fits, he made sure that I knew how to give him CPR and use a GPS locater do get help, if needed. We continued our adventures for a long time. One day we were out in the backcountry just fishing, and he had a heart attack. I did what he had taught me. I called for help with the Garmin and started CPR. I guess I did OK—he lived. We went out many more times after that. I guess it was all part of the plan. It was meant to be. From that day forward, I knew what I was going to do."

Faith found herself staring into Tad's eyes, not sure how to respond. "Your grandfather must have been a great person," she finally said. "You know, I'm not sure I have ever had that kind of ah-hah moment, unless you count my last boyfriend. I knew when it was time to get out."

"Did that moment propel you towards something?"

Faith had not thought of it that way, but she was a bit shocked when she realized that it had bought her here, to this small mountain town, to this hospital, and to this hospital cafeteria.

"Yes, in fact, it did."

"There you go."

Faith grabbed the brown bag that still contained french fries and took a few more. "Have you ever been to this?" she asked Tad, pointing to a flyer that was stapled to the paper bag.

Tad grabbed the bag to take a closer look. "The music festival. I have always wanted to go, but I'm always tied up when it rolls around."

"I would like to go," said Faith.

"We should do that. Why don't you ask me to go? After all, I can provide the transportation."

Faith looked at Tad, not knowing where this conversation was going.

"You have to ask me. Doctor and patient relations."

Faith smiled. "So, that's how this works. Well, Doctor Stephens, would you like to take me out to the music festival this weekend?"

"Yes, I would. By the way, it's Tad."

"Nope. Doctor-patient relations, Doctor Stephens." They both laughed.

"I guess it's a date." Tad was amused at how things had worked out. "Let's get you moved over to the lodge. I'll go get my truck and pull up front. See if Alice can get us a cart to move all the flower vases." With that, he was off, and Faith headed back to her room.

"Alice, what am I going to do with all these flowers?"

Alice skipped the question. "I think Doctor Stephens has a thing for you, Faith."

"I'm sure he is like that with all of his patients."

"No, not really." Faith had known Alice for only a few days, but she was not one to beat around the bush. Faith thought that maybe there was something there.

"Alice, do you think Mr. Wells would be offended if I didn't take all these flowers?"

"Not at all. He is not like that, and besides, he sent these over to brighten your days while you were in the hospital."

"They did help, but you and the staff are the real reason I felt comfortable and taken care of. Thank you for that."

"I'm so happy to hear that. That it is what we are supposed to do."

"Let's load up the birds of paradise, and you and the staff can split up the rest. Use them in your homes. Perhaps you will get the same pleasure they gave me."

Alice and Faith headed down the hall with the birds of paradise towards the entrance. Tad was there waiting. "Alice, thanks again for everything," Faith said.

"Please stop by and say hello before you leave town," Alice said to Faith. "It would make our day. With winter coming on, we would love to see your bright and shiny face again."

They hugged, and then Faith was in the truck and on her way.

Chapter 11:
Fun and Love

Faith stared out the window of her room. The lodge provided the warmth and privacy that she had not had at the hospital. It was shaping up to be a beautiful fall day. The early snowstorm that greeted her when she arrived that first night had all but disappeared. Unfortunately, it had taken the colors of fall from the aspen trees. The leaves now lay upon the ground. As she stepped outside her room and into the sunshine, she was greeted by a warming day. The mornings were now consistently cold, but every few days the sun came out in full force, and the wind died down. The reward was welcome by all, especially this time of the year.

Fun and Love

Days like this would be much harder to come by in the near future and would soon be all but gone until spring.

She could see Tad's truck pulling in. She now recognized it, as they had met several times over the last few days. They ate several dinners together, as his work schedule kept him busy most of the day. She spent that time at the library, still trying to find any information about her dad. Today, however, they would spend the whole day together.

"You better grab your coat. It may be warm now, but later it will be cold," Tad said. Faith went back in and grabbed her coat. She hesitated a minute thinking that she might show Tad the contents of the cookie tin but decided it would be their day. No distractions.

She grabbed her coat and they were off. "I can see why you love this place," Faith said. "It's full of beauty. You never know what will surprise you next. You might see an elk around the next bend, or a deer at the next turn in the river."

"It never gets old," he agreed. "Even in the winter, a fresh snowfall will offer up a completely different landscape from the snowfall of only a few days before. I don't know how long you are planning on staying, but I wish you would stay through the winter. It's a bit of a challenge, with the snow and bitter cold, but it's ski season. Do you ski?"

"I have never tried. It looks like fun, though." Faith looked upon the river below her. She imagined what it would look like after a heavy snowstorm. She started to realize that as wonderful as it was, she could not live off Mr. Wells' generosity forever. If she were to stay, she would have to find a place and a job. She had no idea how she could make a living here. She was so engrossed in trying to figure out how to make it work here that she missed what Tad was saying.

"Faith? Faith?"

"I'm sorry. What were you asking?"

"Would you like me to teach you?"

"Teach me what?"

"To ski." They had stopped, so Tad made eye contact with her. "I don't want to scare you off or jump to any conclusions, but I really like you. I would like to spend more time with you. I don't want you to leave. I realize this may sound a bit selfish, because I'm not sure why you're here or what your plans are, but if you're open to it, I would like to see where this could go. I know that what's happening here, between us, was nothing that either of us had planned, but the way I see it, this is the way things are meant to be. We don't know why, but two people collide, and suddenly life grabs you and whisks you in a direction you never expected. I would like to see where this path leads—see if this is meant to be. I'm sorry, I'm probably moving too fast."

Faith clicked her seat belt off and kissed Tad before she even realized that she had done so. She held on, not wanting to break the emotions of the moment. She looked into Tad's eyes. "I have no idea where this is going, but right now I'm loving every minute I'm with you," she said as she kissed him again.

A car pulled up behind them at the stop sign and sounded the horn. "Right now, let's not make any plans. Let's just go enjoy the day. Let's see what transpires,"

Faith said. They got in one last embrace before relenting to the driver behind them.

As they made their way to the music festival, Faith remained next to Tad. Sitting next to him seemed right. She felt like she was exactly where she was supposed to be.

They finally arrived. A parking space was hard to come by, but Faith refused to be dropped off at the entrance gate. "I can walk. Besides, I want to walk with you." They found a spot, and both exited the driver's side. Tad closed the car door and immediately pushed her against the truck in another emotional embrace.

"Get a room," a bystander quipped.

They looked at each other and laughed. "Let's go hear some music."

The day was wonderful for both. They enjoyed every performer. They found many songs they loved. They ate, they drank, they sang along, they danced, and they stayed close.

On the way back to the lodge, Faith continued to ride by Tad's side.

Tad pulled in near her room. "I should walk you in, but I'm not going to. I don't trust myself right now. I don't want to rush these feelings I have for you."

"I don't trust myself, either. I might rip off all your clothes before I could unlock the door," Faith said, smiling. She laid both hands on either side of Tad's face and pulled him close. "Thank you, Doctor Stephens, for this day. It was wonderful!" She gave Tad a quick kiss on the lips and exited the passenger-side door.

He opened his door and stood on the step rail. "I want to take you on an adventure this week. I'm off on Wednesday. It's my favorite spot in this whole mountain range. Can you make it?"

"Let me check my schedule," said Faith with a sly smile. "Of course, I can make it!"

"One more thing, Faith. Can you blink your porch light twice once you have checked things inside? It would make me feel a lot better since I'm not coming in."

Faith blew him a kiss before she stepped inside, and the porch light blinked twice within a minute.

Tad sat in his truck, staring at Faith's door, reliving the day they'd had. He smiled, started the engine, and drove off, daydreaming of the next time he would see her.

They kept their date on Wednesday, but Tad postponed the adventure he had promised Faith. The weather had turned a little cooler; frequent shifts were common this time of year. Instead, they spent the day in a nearby town, enjoying the time together while shopping and eating at new locations.

Tad dropped her off at the lodge once again, after their adventures that day. She blinked the porch light twice. This had become a habit. This night, however, she found a note that had been slid under her door. The note was from the lodge. The lodge informed her that they needed to do some maintenance in her room starting Thursday.

The next morning, she went straight to the lodge office to get more details. The staff asked if she could move down a couple of doors. She was happy to comply. She and Tad would not get together today. This gave her time to move her things and make it to the library once again. It worked out great, as Tad had arranged for his shift to get covered on Friday, and the weather was supposed to be better.

Chapter 12:
No Sale

"Good morning," Keith announced to the staff as he passed through to his office. "Dan, can you stop by when you have a minute?"

"Sure thing," Dan responded. "I'll stop in when I finish this project."

The employees of Wells Mill and Lumber had voted unanimously for a "no sale" to the offer that Keith had presented. Keith was proud of them. He knew that this company was a vital part of the town, and if the sale had gone through, many of his employees may have lost their jobs—or they may have shut down the place all together. He missed out on a lot of money, and many of employees did as well, but he thought of the adage, "A bird in hand is better than two in the bush." The vote also reaffirmed his faith in humanity. His team had put family and community among their top priorities. That's why he loved this place and the people.

It also meant that he would have something to occupy his time. He was afraid of loneliness. His job was his family. It had also been a part of his family's life, until the passing of his wife and daughter. After their deaths, he avoided going into town when it could be avoided, and he didn't go out much, unless it was with the group of guys he'd grown up with. They had started getting together for breakfast on Saturdays.

He even changed his routine of going to the grocery store. Invariably, he would be stopped two or three times by someone he knew, and sometimes by even those he didn't know. They'd always say the same thing: "We're so sorry for your loss." That did fade over time, but then they would ask, "How are you?" It was an innocent enough question, and a typical one, but to Keith it was a reminder. A reminder of his loss.

A reminder of that day the police officers stood in his doorway. They could have been there for any number of reasons, but that day, it was the worst possible reason. He knew it when he opened the door. The officers had had their hats in hands, and their body language had instantly made him nauseous. Keith had said nothing. He hadn't been able to find the words or the courage to move the conversation. It had been as if, if he didn't ask, then he didn't know. He would surely wake up from a bad dream.

He just quit interacting with the public when possible. He didn't need their pity. He needed space. He didn't blame them for asking questions. They were trying to show empathy. He knew it was how he translated the interaction, but he didn't know how to fix it. He knew he must find a way to move on. He couldn't shake the feeling that he was a sailboat with no sail, destined to drift aimlessly across the ocean. He only found his sail when he was with Keiko or at work.

A friend of his dad's helped him find paddles for his sailboat. He had come by the house on a random visit, a year after he had lost his family. He'd given him a book about the history of the area they lived in, which was rich in Native Indian history. The book took a high-level look at the local history, giving context for many of the areas that he had come across in all his years growing up in the area. However, it raised more questions than it provided answers, which set him on a journey from one book to another. He became engrossed with history and of the people who once called this area home. Keiko spent many days beside Keith's desk as he poured through books and articles.

Eventually, the books drove him from the house and library and into the land outside for more answers.

When the day came for Keith to move the research outdoors, Keiko became a happier dog. She always knew when an adventure was going to happen. She would run toward the door and then back at Keith. She would bark at him. She would sit in front of him, tail wagging, but not for long. Then she would run towards the door again. When Keith finally grabbed the leash, she would turn in circles. Keith was never sure if it was due to Keiko's intuition or if it had just become his routine on those mornings. All he knew was that Keiko's excitement was contagious.

He spent many a weekend tracking down clues pointing to ancient villages and camps. Although he hadn't found the places he was looking for, he was outside. It distracted his mind. He was away from the house. He escaped the memories.

Keith was still determined to find some of those lost villages referred to in his research. He had visited many areas in the past but had always come up emptyhanded. There were still lots of areas on his list. He was in the middle of daydreaming about his next search area when Dan stopped by and knocked.

"Keith, do you have time to talk now?"

"Sure, come on in, and take a seat." Keith went through some small talk about family and weekend plans until he got around to the real purpose of the conversation.

"Dan, how's your side business doing?"

Dan had been building furniture on the side for several years. He mainly built furniture based on specific requests from co-workers, friends, and family.

"It's going good. It pays the Christmas bills every year. I enjoy doing it. Do you need me to make you a piece?"

Keith thought a minute before responding. "Actually, I need you to make a lot of pieces—and all different types. We all decided not to sell this company. We discussed the idea that the company that wanted to buy us would probably purchase our competitor if we did not sell. I still expect that to happen. So, we need to change. I would like to see Wells Mill and Lumber become a furniture manufacturer. I need somebody that is familiar with constructing furniture to help us make that change. If you're interested, I would like to make you my vice president. You will oversee design and training. You will have me to help with organization and equipment acquisition. It's a big responsibility. I have chosen you because of your background in this area and the respect and admiration every employee has for you. The position will come with a raise and bonuses. What do you think?"

By the time Keith had finished, Dan was on the edge of his chair. "I'm going to say absolutely, but it wouldn't be right not to ask my wife for her thoughts. Can I let you know tomorrow?"

"Not a problem, Dan. Let's revisit this when we get back in the morning. Can you keep this between you and me and Doris until you make a decision and I make the announcement?"

"You bet," said Dan. "I'll make sure Doris does the same."

Chapter 13: Crises

Friday arrived, and it turned out to be a beautiful day, just as promised. Faith decided to walk to Tad's house versus him picking her up. She wanted to enjoy the weather and see more of the area, so she set out on foot.

Bringing her coat had turned out to be a good move. The morning was still chilly, and the shady spots were even colder.

She had been to Tad's house a few times but had never really been inside for any length of time.

Tad was in his driveway, doing something in his truck when Faith walked up.

"I'm here reporting for the big adventure, Captain."

Tad smiled. "So, you did walk. How was it?"

"It was spectacular."

"It's a good warm-up for what I have in store for today. We will do some driving, some hiking, some eating, and other than that, a bit of relaxing."

"Let's stop by the grocery store for drinks and stuff," Faith suggested.

"Already done and packed."

Faith looked in the truck. "I don't see anything."

"No truck today." Faith looked at Tad, trying to figure out what she had signed up for. "As your captain today, I suggest you suit up, sailor."

"Tad, what have you got me into?" Faith was starting to get a little nervous. "Why do I need a uniform?"

Tad reached in the cab of the truck and produced a ball cap. "What are you worried about? It's just a cap." He smiled.

"So, this is the uniform?"

"Yes—well, almost." Tad put the cap on Faith's head backward, gave her a big kiss, and walked over to the garage. "Now for our ship," he said as he stepped into the garage. He backed out a Jeep, no top, and no doors.

Faith was elated. "I have always wanted to ride in a Jeep." She looked inside, and sure enough, it was packed with blankets, a cooler, and picnic supplies. "It's so tall, how am I supposed to get in?" she asked. Tad reached in the cab and flipped a switch and down came a step rail. She got in, and Tad took his seat.

"One more item." He handed her headphones with a microphone attached. "We can talk and use these to listen to music today." He put his headphones on, and they were off.

They talked a lot on the first part of trip—unless Tad had a favorite song, then he sang. If Faith knew the song, she sang along. The music tended to override the microphone, so she thought she was safe singing along.

They eventually turned off on a dirt road. "Should we take off the headphones?" Faith asked.

"Not yet, but shortly. Can you do me a favor? Switch my playlist. Change it to *Instrumental*," Tad said. The music fit the moment.

The Story of Faith

At first, the scenery was uneventful, but the elevation started changing. They started pulling out of the high desert and climbing. It became cooler. The dusty air of a few miles back succumbed to a light sprinkle of rain. The drops collected the dust particles and freshened the air. The vegetation soon turned from brush to evergreen. The embankment along the road now rose on either side of the road, dominated by what appeared to be granite cliffs. The grass turned from sparse to deep green, thick and plentiful, and a river now cut through the narrow valley they were now driving through. The river was powerful and flowing fast, but not deep. It poured over boulders and through trees and brush that sometimes hid the water. It was a treasure, and it was all theirs today.

"Can we stop here?" she asked.

"Do you need to go to the restroom?"

"Actually, yes."

"That's fine. I'll pull over just ahead."

Tad pulled over. They took their headphones off, and the sound of the river rushing through the valley and over the rocks now dominated. The slight wind blowing through the nearby pines gave the whole scene a relaxing vibe. Faith sat there for a minute, taking it all in. "This place is unbelievable."

"And there is more to come."

"How can it get any better?"

"I have two more places I would like to show you today. Each has its own brand of spectacular." He reached into the back seat and produced a roll of toilet paper. "You might need this. Do you know the best part about the restrooms out here? Besides the beauty and fresh air? You can go anywhere you like," he said with a smile.

Faith took off for a clump of trees, and Tad did his business beside the Jeep.

Faith was returning to the Jeep but got just close enough to chuck the toilet paper roll to Tad. "I'm going down by the river."

Tad watched as she plowed through the knee-high verdant grass towards the river. He thought about how happy he was that this girl had landed in his life. He was so impressed by her sense of adventure. She was always all in, with everything they did.

He started thinking of other girls he had dated. They usually lost interest long before the dirt road hit the river, and he never got past the second stop with any of them. Faith was different. She was meant to be here today, with him, and on this trip. He could feel it. It felt right.

Faith was yelling his name. The river drowned out her words, but he could tell she was motioning for him to come down to the river, so that's where he went.

"Look what I found!" She pointed along the river's edge. Lying before them, hidden by the tall grass, was a very large rock, flattened by many years of water rushing over its top. Faith put her arms behind Tad's neck. "Promise that you will bring me back here, to this rock, for lunch during the spring." Tad didn't even answer. They fell into each other arms, and this kiss would have lasted forever if it hadn't been interrupted by three ducks that had been hiding in the eddy just over the lip of the river bank. They made quite a commotion when they took flight. Faith and Tad looked at each other and had a laugh.

"I promise we will be back here together, on this rock, beside this river, with the best picnic ever."

They walked hand in hand back to the Jeep and continued their trip up the dirt road, headphones off, enjoying the symphony all around them.

The next few miles were a little more difficult, as the terrain got rockier and steeper. They were definitely going up. Faith reached into the back seat and grabbed her jacket. As they went up, the temperature went down.

"How far are we going?" Faith asked.

"To the top. And we are almost there."

"Good! It's getting scary." They had been on switchbacks for last few miles. Sometimes Tad was looking down and over a drop-off, and sometimes it was Faith looking at disaster if they were to veer off course. The only thing she could think about was her last visit to the hospital. A trip over the side here and the hospital would not be an option.

"Hey, Tad? Why don't you drive as far to the left as possible? This is making me lightheaded when I'm looking over the edge."

The Story of Faith

They finally seemed to level off, and the back and forth across the side of the mountain ended, much to Faith's relief. Tad didn't seem to be alarmed by the terrain, but Faith being new on this road, had no idea what lay around the next bend or rise in the road. Tad's confidence gave her some comfort, as he seemed to know where he was going.

The trees opened to reveal a wide-open rocky plateau that was the size of several football fields. Faith realized why this place was special to Tad. The grandeur could only be appreciated by being there and seeing it with your own eyes. The whole state seemed to lay in front of them, whether you looked left, right, straight, or behind you. There were valleys and peaks in all directions. From this vantage point, they were the only two people in the whole world.

Tad said nothing. He shut the engine off and got out. Faith followed him. "Wow, I can't believe the view up here," she said.

Tad grabbed binoculars from the cab of the Jeep. "Come sit on the bumper with me." Faith sat beside him on the front of the Jeep and put her arms around his waist for a little extra warmth. "Here," said Tad, "take these binoculars and look at that area where the trees seem a bit spotty." He pointed. "See if you can find it without the binoculars first."

It took Faith some time to realize she needed to look beyond what was near and focus on what was distant. She found the spot where the last of the mountains met the horizon. Then she found the valley and the open area. She used the binoculars to bring the view closer in. "Is that a town?"

"That is a town. It's our town. The town we left earlier."

Faith just smiled in disbelief. "Wow, unbelievable!"

"See what else you can find. I'm going to get lunch set out."

Faith explored the whole area with the binoculars. She found other towns, spotted a road or two, even a lake, before bringing her thoughts back to the area she and Tad occupied in this vast expanse of wilderness. She took the binoculars from her eyes and found Tad on a blanket, leaning back and soaking up the sun. Everything was set out.

"Come sit," he said.

"Tad, thank you for this—for all of this. Thanks for bringing me to such a special place. You are such a good host. Thank you for everything. Thank you for taking care of me. You're the best thing that has happened to me in a long time."

"You better eat something. I have one more place to show you, and we are going to have to hike to get there. You will need the energy."

They talked and laughed through the entire lunch. They finally took a seat on a large rock to rest before the next leg of their journey and to take in the sights on top of their world.

Silence finally found its way into their conversation. It didn't interrupt their connection, however. Two people couldn't get much closer. They were together, sharing and enjoying the peace and serenity of the view.

"This is a miracle," Tad finally said. Faith could feel the emotion emanating from him. "This place, this moment, and us, Faith. Think of all the things that led us to be here, today, together. How many random acts came together to bring us to where we are right now? How can moments like this be just pure happenstance? If you hadn't made that trip the night you did. Wrecked your car and been rescued. Come into the hospital the night I was taking call." Tad turned and faced Faith, took her hands in his, and looked into her eyes. "I believe this was meant to be. I think we are exactly where we should be."

Faith stared into Tad's eyes until she could no longer resist. She slowly made her way to his lips.

"Can we stay here? In this moment, forever?" she finally asked.

"It's ours. We have it forever. We can relive it again, and replay it anytime, from now to eternity."

Together, they broke down their picnic and packed it away.

"OK, last adventure of the day. Are you still up to it?" Tad asked.

"I feel like I'm on top of the world." They both broke out in laughter.

Back at the Jeep, Tad packed a backpack. "I have drinks and snacks if we need them.

It's not far, but we might need some of this on the way back," he said as he tied up the backpack and slung it over his shoulder. "You will also need some equipment." He reached into the back of the Jeep.

"What kind of equipment?" Faith was a bit startled with the possibilities.

Tad didn't respond. He just produced a hiking stick from the back. "Here you go," he said with a smile, as he handed the stick to Faith.

"Whew, thank goodness. I thought you were going to hand me rope and carabiners."

"What do you know about climbing?" Tad said with a surprised grin. "I was saving that for next trip." He pulled back a blanket in back to reveal climbing rope and carabiners.

"Oh, no. I had all I wanted of that back in college."

Tad shut the Jeep and they started walking. "I'm impressed. Tell me about it."

"There is not much to tell. I took a backpacking class. We had to choose between camping and rappelling for our final grade. I would have rather gone camping, but none of the dates on the schedule matched up, so I got stuck with rappelling."

"Wow, that must have been awesome!"

"It was the scariest thing I've ever done. We went to a fire training center. They had a building that was five stories tall, and we rappelled off the roof. I made it to the edge, no problem, but taking that first step over—that was a mental challenge. My mind kept telling my feet not to do it, but I finally made it, with lots of coaxing from the instructor."

The trail they were on soon intersected with a river. "OK, so we are going to follow this trail downstream to this place I want you to see. Keep in mind we are going down the trail, so that means to get back to the Jeep we must come back up the trail. Let's take our time and save our energy for the return." With that, they followed the river down.

The trail eventually veered off from the river, and they proceeded down some steep and rocky terrain. "We are about there," Tad said.

The trail took a turn through a thick grove of pine trees, and then the trees opened to reveal a scene like nothing Faith had ever seen. The river they had followed was now spilling over a cliff 100 feet above them. The water, a collage of white and blue, fell in front of them like a stampede of horses.

Neither said a word as they took in the creation in front of them. Faith took Tad's hand, and they walked even closer. They were just close enough to feel the temperature drop as the mist stuck to the air and enveloped them.

"Our summers up here above eight thousand feet never get too hot, but this would still feel good on a bright sunny day. This can be another trip for us next summer," he added.

They turned and walked away, but Faith stopped for one last look before entering the tree line again. She didn't say anything, but thought to herself: *I will be back.*

They made it back to the end of the dirt road just as it got dark. Tad stopped the Jeep and got out to pull a heavy blanket out of the back. "We are only a little way from town, but it might get cold." He covered Faith with the blanket and they headed back to town.

Crises

Faith was growing tired from a day full of adventure. "Take me to your house," she told Tad. She donned the headphones, put on Tad's instrumental selection again, and pulled the blanket tight around her neck.

Tad hadn't even gotten up to the posted speed on the highway before she was asleep. He looked over at his sleeping beauty many times on the ride home. He couldn't remember a time that he had been happier.

The music had kept Faith asleep for the ride home, but the start, stop, and turns of the Jeep broke through the hypnosis of the ride, and she began to stir as they pulled into the drive. As the Jeep came to a stop, she looked over at Tad, who had a panicked look on his face. She removed her headphones. "What is it?" she asked.

Tad still had a panicked look. "Shit! Stay here," he told her.

Tad had not even put two feet on the ground before a blonde girl appeared from inside of his garage.

Faith, who was now out of the Jeep, caught the attention of the girl.

"I should have known you were seeing someone else! Did you tell her about us?" the girl asked.

"Don't do this again," Tad said quickly. He looked at Faith, not prepared for the situation he now found himself in. "Faith, this is not what you think."

The girl was quick to respond. "I bet he took you to all of his favorite places in the mountains today. Just like he does all of his latest bad habits!"

The girl obviously meant something to Tad, and her slurred speech led Faith to believe she had probably had too much to drink. The combination of her intoxication, Tad's loss for words, and the sneak attack she was enduring sent Faith fleeing.

She heard Tad yelling as she fled. "Faith! Don't leave, I can explain. Faith! Faith!"

She ran. She cried. She couldn't make sense of what happened because her heart was hurting so bad. Still sobbing, she finally came to a stop and immediately became nauseous. She stumbled around with her head down, not knowing where she was going, reliving all the happy moments she'd had with Tad, and each time the girl's screaming, ranting face turned the whole memory into a living hell.

Had she let love make a fool out of her? Was she so blinded that she couldn't see that she was being manipulated? These questions and many more repeated over and over in her head till she found herself back at her room at the lodge.

Her key was not working, adding to her frustration. She was standing outside her door, completely lost. She didn't know left from right, up from down, or front from back. A voice broke through her confused and obliterated state of mind. "Ms. Jones, are you OK?" At first, she did not pick up on the direction of the voice. "Are you OK?" came the voice again. She realized it was coming from the direction of the office.

She wiped away her tears and cleared her throat before responding. "Yes, fine. I'm just having trouble with my key."

"Don't forget, we changed your room," said the voice.

"Of course. Sorry, I completely forgot. It's been a long day."

With that, she headed to her new room. She felt tied and bound, with a lack of direction. She was lost in thought. What had seemed so clear, so right, so meant to be just an hour ago, was now a forest with no road out.

Chapter 14:
The Return of George

Faith had packed her things and checked out. After last night, she had decided to head back home, and a job would go a long way toward getting her back on her feet. The whole ordeal with Tad and his girlfriend or fiancé—whatever she was to him—was a real punch in the gut. The flowers and card she saw a few doors down from her room this morning only reminded her of what she thought she had.

She decided to stop by the diner and get breakfast before she left town. A cup of coffee would help keep her awake after her restless night. She loved the diner, no matter what time of day. It was perfect for this slow-paced community. It was one of the few places she had ever eaten where the food was fresh and freshly prepared. No frozen items would be served here. There was a price to pay though: you better have some time. She took a seat at a booth just beyond the front door, three booths down.

Faith took in the smell of the fresh bread being baked. She had to turn away from the pie behind the glass case. She thought she should get a slice with all she had been through the last several weeks. *I should order the whole pie.* She had come out in search of her dad but ended up in the hospital, without a car, and on top all that, she had a broken heart. She had looked at some high school yearbooks at the library, but with just the name of Flash, it had been a fruitless search.

The waitress made it over finally. "What can I get you this morning, darling?"

"What are those gentlemen having over there?" asked Faith. She was looking at a table of eight middle-aged men having breakfast. They looked like they had known each other forever the way they were laughing and carrying on. In fact, Mr. Wells was one of the eight.

The waitress took a glance. "They are having our strawberry crepes."

Faith thought a moment. "I'll have that too. Since I'm skipping the pie this morning, I might as well."

The waitress agreed, "You only live once. As you can see, I take full advantage of that saying." The waitress laughed at herself, but Faith could only manage a slight smile.

She gave the waitress her menu and glanced back over at the table of men. She was in the middle of contemplating the idea that one of them might know of, or be, her dad. They looked to be the right age.

The bell on the door rang as it always did when a customer entered, only this time the bell was different. It wasn't the bell ringing that interrupted her thought. It was the interruption in conversation. All eyes glanced at the door. She turned and glanced over her shoulder toward the door. She was startled, as she quickly realized it was no stranger. It was George! She wanted to turn and look away, but it was too late—their eyes had already met. Her stomach suddenly got queasy and she became lightheaded. She could not imagine why he had come here, but she knew it wasn't good.

Faith starred at George as he made his way over to her table. "Hey George," she said. He didn't respond as he made his way to the other side of her table. "Would you like to sit down?" she asked.

George skipped the pleasantries and got right to the point. "I'm here to bring you home!" he said rather rudely. Faith was over her anxiousness. "I have a bus ticket. I don't need a ride. After what you did, why do you think I would ever ride with you or have anything to do with you again?" She wasn't looking for an answer.

He was growing more and more insistent with his request, which now seemed more like a demand.

Keith and his friends had taken note of the developing situation at the booth just down from their table. Keith's lifelong friend Joe was sitting to his right. They both had turned to see what the commotion was about. Joe saw the guy grab the girl's arm

The Return of George

as if he were going to drag her out of the booth. Joe turned toward Keith. "Isn't that the girl—" But Keith was gone. "Oh, shit," Joe said as he whipped his head back toward the booth, just in time to see Keith hit the young man like a linebacker zeroed in on a quarterback from his blindside. The guy went flying and slid from the third booth all the way back to the doorway. As if it were planned, the bell above the door rang, and the sheriff walked in.

The sheriff looked down at the guy at his feet. "Can I help you, son?"

The manager had made his way to the front counter and quickly chimed in. "He just tripped. He's on his way out."

George got up, dusted himself off, and looked in the direction of Faith and Keith, who was now standing by her booth. "You guys be careful!" he said as he left.

The sheriff watched George as he walked out the door. Once the door closed, he looked at Keith inquisitively. "Did he mean you be careful . . . like take of yourself? Or did he mean you be careful . . . like watch your back?"

Keith thought a moment. "I'm not sure. Maybe he thought I tripped him." With that, there were a few giggles, and everybody went back to snickering and talking about the incident.

Keith looked down at Faith. "Sorry, I have a very low tolerance for that kind of behavior. Are you OK? Who is that guy?"

"He's an ex-boyfriend."

Can I sit with you for a minute?" asked Keith.

Faith was glad for Keith's help once again. "Please do sit. I need to settle my nerves. Thanks for bailing me out—again!"

Keith looked at her luggage sitting in the booth beside her. "Are you heading out? You know if you leave I will not be there to help when you get in the next tight spot."

"I thought you and Tad had something going?"

With tears in her eyes, Faith looked down. "Well, I thought he was single, until last night, and his girlfriend showed up."

Keith looked surprised. "Girlfriend? Who was that?"

"I didn't stick around to find out."

The Return of George

Keith thought a minute, "Was she kind of a tall skinny blond with long hair? With a lot of make-up?"

Faith considered his description. "Well, yes, that sounds like what she looked like."

Keith snickered. "That's his ex! She's a real piece of work. Looks like you two need to flee the country and get away from your exes." He laughed. "Don't mind her. She's harmless, and probably already left town and went back home. It seems like anytime Tad starts taking a liking to somebody, she shows up. She must have a spy in town."

Keith laughed again. "I thought you were looking for someone in town. Did you ever find them?"

Faith considered the question while trying to weigh the information Keith had provided about Tad. "Maybe I overreacted last night. Sorry, no, I never found the person I was looking for."

At that, Keith turned to the sheriff at the counter. "Bill!" He waited for Bill to turn around. "This is my friend Faith. She is trying to find an old friend. Do you think you could help her?"

"No problem. Why don't you come by the station after breakfast and we can talk."

"Bill's like me, he has been here forever and knows everybody."

"Thanks, Mr. Wells," Faith said. "Thanks for everything. Thanks for my accommodations at the lodge."

"Faith, it's been a pleasure. I hope you give Tad a second chance. It would be nice to have you stick around our little town. We need a bright and sweet personality around here. It's uplifting."

Faith voiced her disagreement. "I'm not sure about how bright and sweet I am."

Keith thought a moment before responding. "Sure, it's there, Faith—you have it. Don't you see it? I can see it, and I know Tad does. Can I give you a ride anywhere?"

"I'm good, Mr. Wells, but thanks for the offer."

"Very good, hon. Stay away from cars and exes. By the way, you never came out to my house to thank Keiko." Keith pulled his receipt for breakfast from his pocket. and quickly scribbled something on the back.

The Return of George

"I'll be home today if you have time to stop by." He made his way back over to his friends. Faith picked up the receipt and found a map scribbled across the back. At the top it read "Keith Wells Homestead."

Chapter 15:
Finding Direction

Faith had left the diner. The manager had agreed to keep her belongs in the back till she returned, so she took only her drawstring sport pack. She was walking, but she did not know where. She stopped and looked behind her. She started left, then turned back to her right. She had Mr. Wells' invitation. She had the sheriff and his promise to help locate her dad, which was the only reason she was in this town. She had this community. And then, she had Tad. She thought about what Mr. Wells had said about Tad's ex-girlfriend, but she was still perplexed. Why had he not come for her when she'd walked away from his house last night? She sat down on a bench that was close by to sort through things.

The one thing she didn't have was a desire to return home. Yet that was what she was about to do. With the latest escapades by George, she now realized that there was nothing there for her any longer. But she now had no place to go. She had no job. She had no place to stay, since she had checked out of the lodge.

"The lodge!" she said out loud. Those two words finally bought some clarity to her thoughts. She remembered passing by her original room this morning. She remembered the flowers and note at the foot of the door. She was so heartbroken about the way things had ended the night before, she had overlooked those items. Could Tad have left those for her? She never told him that she had switched rooms. She took off running for the lodge. Considering Mr. Wells' insight this morning, she began to tear up with the possibility that Tad had in fact tried to find her. She ran faster, hoping not to lose another chance at the one thing that had given her direction and happiness.

The Story of Faith

As she got closer to the lodge, she looked upon the cars parked out in front of all the doors at the lodge. She so wished they had left this morning, so she could see that door. "Would the flowers and card still be there? Were they left for her?"

They were still there. She began to walk toward them. She approached them slowly and with caution, as if they would bolt like a rabbit if she frightened them. She stood at the door, staring down at the flowers and card. She wiped the tears from her eyes and knelt to pick up the card.

She read her name, and it made her feel as if joy, elation, happiness, and love were all combined into one emotion.

Faith,

I can only hope you will open this and read it. I'm so sorry for last night. That was my ex-girlfriend, and she has a habit of showing up unannounced. I should have told you about her.

I tried to find you last night. I wish we could have talked about this live, but I finally gave in to the notion that you were in your room and did not want to talk with me.

Finding Direction

I can explain everything, but I would rather write about us. You are the best thing that has ever happened to me. I fell in love with you the moment I saw you. It has been pure delight for me to be in your company the last few weeks. I can't get enough. My day is only bright when I have you around. When we are not together, I stare at the clock on my phone, watching the minutes tick by, counting down 'til the moment my eyes see you again. Every night brings heartache because I must leave you once again. I AM IN LOVE WITH YOU, FAITH. Please don't leave without allowing me to apologize.
I'm yours, always,
Tad

Faith started crying again. Tears were spotting the paper as if it were raining. She could not deny the mutual feelings she had for him. She was relieved, knowing that her feelings and intuition were not just wishful thinking. She could see that he cared for real. She realized she was truly in love.

Faith wanted to run to Tad and tell him that she had the same feelings, but she decided to wait. She wanted to put one thing behind her so that she could focus her full attention on their relationship. She had spent many hours in the library trying to gather any kind of direction on who her dad was. She decided to go to this one last source, the sheriff, and give it one more chance.

Faith placed the letter in her drawstring sport pack and dropped the flowers off for the lady at the front desk of the lodge. She then made her way over to the sheriff's office. The lady at the front greeted her as she walked in.

"How can we help you today?"

"I'm looking for the sheriff. He goes by Bill."

A booming voice from the office just off the front entrance spoke out, "Send her back, Sherry. It's a friend of Keith's."

Sherry pointed Faith to Bill's door.

"Come in and have a seat. It's Faith, correct?"

"Yes, sir!"

Bill was larger than life in more than just his bravado. He was seated at his desk, leaning back in his chair with his legs crossed and his boots propped up on a small side table. "Well, Flash says you're trying to find someone?"

"Excuse me?" Faith stood up from the chair, not sure if she had just imagined what she heard.

The sheriff took note of the surprised look on Faith's face. "Flash. Keith. Keith Wells. he says you are looking for someone from here, right?"

Faith stood before the sheriff in disbelief. "So, Mr. Wells' nickname is Flash?" She was stunned to the core.

"Yes, that's correct."

Faith stammered through her next question, which turned into three. "So how, where did he get his nickname? Did he play football? What year did he graduate?"

The sheriff had all the right answers.

Faith dug through the sport pack she had now taken off her back. She found the cookie tin. She opened it and looked at the class ring. It all matched up. She took the photo of Flash out and held it in front of the sheriff.

"Do you know who this is?" she asked.

"Yes, that's Keith. We played together," he responded.

Before the sheriff could finish his next thought, Faith was heading out the door.

"Thanks, Bill," she said on her way out.

"Is that who you were looking for?" he yelled after her.

Her next stop was the hospital. Tad was at the nursing station. His head was buried in a patient's chart. Even though Tad was oblivious, the staff saw her enter. The area grew quiet as Faith approached, which caught the attention of Tad. He first looked at them. Staff members were all singularly focused on one thing. Tad turned his head to discover what. It was Faith. In an instant, his methodical day turned into instant relief and happiness. "Faith, I'm—"

Faith stopped him mid-sentence. "I accept your apology, and I'm so sorry I rushed to judgment. Thank you for the flowers and the card. Can we talk about this tonight? Right now, I need your car."

"Sure, no problem. I brought the Jeep today."

"Thank you. I love you." Faith said as she gave him a big kiss. As she took off, she could hear one person begin to clap, and before she exited the hallway, it sounded like the entire area was applauding.

She jumped into the Jeep and took the map Keith had drawn her and read it again, "Keith Wells Homestead." She was off.

The closer she got to her destination, the more emotional she became. There were so many things coming together at once, she could scarcely stay focused on any one thought for more than a few seconds. As she turned down the lane leading to Keith's driveway, she thought of her mom and what she had sacrificed. The love she had given Faith at the sacrifice of what might have been her mom's one true love. She was sad for her mom but happy that she had shared her past and sent her on this adventure. Her mom would be ecstatic at the way things were turning out.

She thought of Keith. The man who had now rescued her twice. Would he be there for her once again? Was he, in fact, her dad? She truly believed so. She thought about how lost and alone she'd felt this morning: no Mom, no Dad, and no Tad.

Then her thoughts turned to Keith. How had he endured the loss of a wife and daughter yet found peace and purpose? He was still here, waiting for something he didn't even know he had. What kind of force could be at play to give them this chance to meet after life had kept them apart for so many years. *Life is strange and moving*, she thought, as she made the turn into his driveway. She was now overflowing with emotions but didn't give it a second thought.

There he was, sitting on his porch: her dad. She sat in the car for a minute and watched as he stood up and approached the steps leading down to the driveway.

She could see he recognized her. He started waving as she exited the Jeep.

"Hey, you found us, and it looks like you worked things out with Tad," said Keith. Then he noticed her tears. "Faith, what's wrong? Has something happened?"

Faith still stood behind the door of the Jeep, not knowing how to respond. Among the tears came a smile. A smile of relief and happiness. She reached into the passenger seat and grabbed the cookie tin. She finally pulled the words out among all her tears. "Can I show you this?" She held up the cookie tin.

"Sure, come up and sit and tell me what's going on."

Faith said nothing, as she took a seat next to Keith on the steps. He had a towel over his shoulder and offered it to Faith. "We just finished lunch. Sorry, I do not have any Kleenex out here for you. She took it and wiped away her tears.

"Now what is going on?" he asked her.

"No emergencies, Sorry for alarming you, it's just that . . . well, let me show this."

She opened the cookie tin, and Keith peered inside. "Brenda! Where on earth did you find this?"

"My mom, Brenda, gave it to me." Faith needed no more evidence. She wrapped her arms around Keith's neck and began crying again. "I think you are my dad," she whispered.

Keith loosely hugged her, stunned. Then it came to him all at once. The resemblance was undeniable, the fact that she was in town looking for someone, and that she had his class ring and photo—all the things he had given Brenda so many years ago. He pulled her in tight. He began to cry, as all the years of heartbreak and loneliness would now be balanced. He thought about what it would be like having someone in his life, a daughter, after all that he had been through. He hugged Faith like he would never let her go again. It was a miracle. One that he could never have wished for or imagined.

"I need to show you something," Keith finally said. "Wait right here."

Keith hurried into the house. Keiko came out to check on the visitor when the door was opened.

"You must be Keiko?" Faith said. She gave her a big hug. Keiko returned the favor by cleaning up the tears on her cheeks. "Thank you for saving me. I hope we can become good friends."

Keith returned with a cigar box. He opened it to reveal a photo of her mom and Brenda's high school class ring.

Finding Direction

"We promised each other that we would trade these items and hold on to them until we could reunite. I tried to find her for many years. I even looked again, a few years after my first wife passed, but no luck."

"Keith, you know my mom has passed," said Faith. "The last thing she asked me to do was tell you how much she always loved you and that she thought of you every day."

Keith, with tears in his own eyes, took the kitchen towel once again and wiped the tears from Faith's checks. "I would like to catch up on all the years I missed. I want to know everything. I want to know about you. Will you stay with me?"

Chapter 16: Going Home

Keith looked over the hole he had just dug. He had worked up a sweat, and beads were pouring down his forehead, over his eyebrows, and into his eyes. They also ran down the side of his face and dripped off the end of his nose. He didn't bother to keep the sweat out of his eyes. It was of no consequence, considering the moment at hand. He discarded the shovel and stood up to evaluate the empty spot that lay before him and take one more look at the spot and its view of the surrounding area. Even though he would never expect to see any bystanders, he looked around anyway. He needed this moment of privacy.

Going Home

He took the blanket and fell to his knees over the hole, gently setting it down inside the pit. He stayed on his knees, placing both hands on the dirt at the edge of the hole, looking down upon the blanket. Tears began running down his cheeks, dripping onto the blanket. He sat back on his heels and placed his hands on his thighs.

"Well, I hope you like this spot? It's got a great view, Keiko. You can see our house up on the hill. You can have this great view of all the places you loved to explore." Keith took a deep breath, trying to relax the tightness in his throat so he could continue. It took several deep breaths before he could. "I'm not sure if dogs go to heaven or not, but I'm hoping they do. I need you to find Carli and our little princess and let them know I'm OK. Tell them I love them and tell them they have a half-sister and stepdaughter. Let them know how wonderful she is. Keiko, thanks for everything." Keith had to stop there before continuing. His emotions hindered his ability to talk, but he stayed there over Keiko. He still needed to finish his goodbye.

The Story of Faith

"Thank you for keeping me company all these years. You saved me, one day at a time, and day after day. Keiko, thank you for saving my daughter, Faith." The tears started flowing again, as he thought about the life-changing events that had started that snowy night just a few weeks ago. "You are my hero and savior. I love you girl!"

Keith sat there on his heels, looking down at the blanket till he had no more tears to share. He finally stood up, picked up the shovel, and managed a smile. "I'll be watching over you from the porch on those quiet snowy nights that you loved. I'll make sure the wildflowers of spring decorate you, and I'll make sure the grass doesn't get too tall in the summer so that you can feel the cool afternoon showers. Goodbye, old friend."

Keith had finished covering Keiko's grave and was back on his hands and knees smoothing the surface when Faith pulled up in the driveway in Tad's Jeep. Keith dusted himself off and used his shirt tail to wipe his face.

Faith, who had exited the Jeep, had stopped about halfway down the hill from the house to wait on Keith. "I'm sorry about Keiko," she said as Keith approached.

"It's a sad day, but she had a good life," Keith said to Faith as he gave her a hug. Keith put his arm around Faith as they turned toward the house. "I guess it was her time. She did what she was supposed to do, completed her mission, and was called home. I can't help but wonder if we don't all have a purpose to fulfill. Keiko was there for me when times were hard and full of heartache. She kept my head up, and then one day she delivered you into my life. I will never forget that. You just never know, so you must trust that there is a plan and meaning to everything. Like your name, you must have faith in your purpose. Now let's go look at those design ideas you put together for our furniture at Wells Mill and Lumber."

Keith turned and took one last look down the hill before entering the house. He couldn't remember a time when the pine trees had looked greener and the sky bluer.

The End

The Story of Faith

Going Home

The Story of Faith